Cupids

Aug. 28/10

To Raymond,
A small reminder
of our wonderful
trip to Nfld.
Happy Birthday
Love
Eric x.

BOOKS BY PAUL BUTLER

St. John's: City of Fire

Rogues and Heroes
(co-author)

Stoker's Shadow

Easton's Gold

NaGeira

Easton

1892

Cupids

a novel

PAUL BUTLER

BRAZEN BOOKS
ST. JOHN'S
2010

Library and Archives Canada Cataloguing in Publication

Butler, Paul, 1964-
  Cupids / Paul Butler.

ISBN 978-1-897317-62-4

  1. Guy, John, d. 1629--Fiction. 2. Merchants--Newfoundland
and Labrador--History--17th century--Fiction. 3. Cupids (N.L.)--
History--17th century--Fiction. 4. Newfoundland and Labrador--
Colonization--Fiction. 5. Newfoundland and Labrador--History--
To 1763--Fiction. I. Title.

PS8635.I355B33 2008   C813'.6   C2008-904360-X

PRINTED IN CANADA

Mixed Sources
Cert no. SW-COC-001271
© 1996 FSC
FSC

This text of this book is printed on Ancient
Forest Friendly paper, FSC certified, that is
chlorine-free and 100% post-consumer waste.

Cover Design: Adam Freake

FLANKER PRESS
PO BOX 2522, STATION C
ST. JOHN'S, NL, CANADA
TOLL FREE: 1-866-739-4420
WWW.FLANKERPRESS.COM

14 13 12 11 10   1 2 3 4 5 6 7 8 9

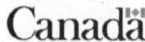 

We acknowledge the financial support of the Government of Canada through the Book
Publishing Industry Development Program (BPIDP) for our publishing activities; the
Canada Council for the Arts which last year invested $20.1 million in writing and pub-
lishing throughout Canada; the Government of Newfoundland and Labrador,
Department of Tourism, Culture and Recreation.

For Maura & Jemma

"My mine of precious stones, my empery;
How am I blest in thus discovering thee!"

Elegy XX by John Donne

CHAPTER ONE

John Guy

September 25, 1611, Cupers Cove

To Sir Willoughby, Mr. Egret, and the most honourable members of the Newfoundland Company of Bristol and London . . .

It is my great pleasure to inform you, sirs, that after one more brief expedition to the northern coast I will begin preparations to return to England for the winter, and that I could not be happier and more secure about the morale of the men and their fitness, under my surrogate, Colston, to continue the good work of fishing, nurturing our beasts, and growing our crops. Through much hard work and diligence we have tilled the soil, raised many root-crops and some grain, and this not without some setbacks. One of the wine barrels was breached somewhat mysteriously last month and there has been some talk of items going astray. Worse than this, a fire last evening did ravage the grain with which we hoped to feed our livestock over the winter, a blow most bitter, but one our men took in great and fine spirits. In all such matters, indeed, I am proud of the good fellowship. We are inured to suffering and to the meagre and uncertain provisions of the pioneer. We will, as always, make do.

I myself, God willing, shall be most delighted to apprise those of you who will be in residence in the fair and beloved city of Bristol of the needs and necessities as well as the good work of my men. I understand that you, Sir Willoughby, will be travelling in foreign parts, and wish you Godspeed and a safe return. I pray that I may beg the indulgence of Mr. Egret and other of your most worthy gentlemen in your absence.

Rest assured, good sirs, despite hardships and uncertainties, the good Christian fellowship and, I humbly trust, my own example and leadership have kept any unrest at bay and it is a perpetual pleasure to see the harmony . . .

CUPIDS

A scuffling noise halts my scratching pen. Two loud thumps follow, then a rough yell, and my door bursts open to the night, almost wrenching the hinge clean away. Writhing inside the burly grasps of Colston and Littlejohn, is Bartholomew, our apprentice cook and gardener. The three enter like a clump of mating insects. When the young man sees me, he ceases to struggle. In the wavering light of the candle, his pale eyes gaze at me with the kind of pleading I have seen only in dogs — not tinged by the slightest suggestion of pride, or even embarrassment, simply intent upon whatever morsel of comfort or sustenance it hopes to receive.

"He was hiding under the wharf," Colston growls, his exposed forearm flexing as Bartholomew makes one futile lurch to the side, a gesture made more for effect and sympathy, I suspect, than for any serious attempt at escape. "What are you going to do with him?" Colston grits his teeth and his strong thumb burrows into the soft flesh of Bartholomew's shoulder.

As though reluctant to believe in the intrusion, my fingers finally allow the quill to drop to the table. It rolls once, feathers nestling against the paper.

"I'll have to bring him back with me once I have completed northern explorations next month. That's laid down."

I notice the hint of relief in the boy's expression.

"We should deal with it here and now, sir," Littlejohn says, his flint-like eyes catching mine. "We have proof he burned the grain. No one would blame us, or even care."

The pleading look returns to those pale eyes which

glisten now behind a film of moisture. I have been here before with Bartholomew, heard his frantic tales of threats and insinuations by day, molestations by night. Now as then it affects me little. The Company's articles are my only guide. They make no mention of the sins of Sodom.

"No," I say quietly. "He returns with me as the law dictates. I will keep him under my watch until that time. I can assure you he will pay."

CHAPTER TWO

Guy

December 1611

I HEAR THE TELLTALE creak of Bartholomew even before he appears in my cabin entranceway. With his regular features, smooth skin, and the hint of down upon his cheek, he is a neat bird designed for the pleasure of viewing. I narrow my eyes to prevent betraying this thought as he draws closer. I am his jailor and he must not forget it.

The door, fixed open by a taut rope behind Bartholomew, is the only anchored thing in this place. The ocean mocks us all with its constant movement; now that we are in the middle of the Atlantic, stillness is a quality beyond reach, a barely remembered myth from times long past. I, myself, am a jelly of perpetual change. My thoughts reshape themselves so rapidly I scarcely know myself from one moment to the next.

"I wish to thank you, your worship," he says softly.

"You are premature," I reply, returning my gaze to the chart. The stool beneath me groans my discomfort. "I have yet to have the pleasure of any such title. I am mayor of no city, judge of no court. You do wrong to flatter."

"I assure you, Mr. Guy, your worthiness makes you a lord in beneficence."

I slide the ruler from the chart.

"What, specifically, do you wish to thank me for, boy?"

"Why, for unchaining me."

"I had you unchained because sickness undermanned my ship. I needed your hands then, not your tongue now."

"Still, you might have returned me to the hold."

"I only haven't because I may need you once more. In the meantime you can thank me by remaining in the space on this ship which has been designated for you."

"I will do so," he says with a bow and takes a short backward step. "But I wish you to know that I appreciate the difficulty of your position. I do understand the weight of an authority such as yours."

The cabin tips, as does my stomach, and my thoughts scramble against his unwanted empathy, pushing against the trust that would like nothing better than to follow his words like shingle tumbling after a retreating wave.

"No one can appreciate it fully," I reply, glaring at him. Then, as his face remains on mine, retaining respect and sympathy in equal measure, I find anger sliding from my visage like an ill-fitting mask. "Leading a group of forty men, my lad, without justice or judge, scaffold or lash, for fifteen months or more, is a trying test for the greatest of men. I believe myself humble enough to admit that I am not the greatest of men."

Where did this come from? I am surely not asking this lad for sympathy. Like the prick of a spear applied to a bulging sack of wine, Bartholomew's words have teased forth emotion that I am at pains to disguise. Fifteen months of grinding work, of encouraging men when I myself feel discouraged, of rewarding the faithful, of punishing miscreants, and settling petty scores with an even hand. And all the while the Company's expectations on my shoulders like some great harness, demanding the incompatible twins of self-sufficiency and yield. Harvest fish, crops and grain, breed your animals, explore the interior and test for ores. Limit victuals to bare necessities. Feed yourselves where possible without delving into Company funds. And beyond these many hoops of burning flame shines Eliza, a star which I fear may remain perpetually beyond reach.

"And yet they expect you to be, your many partners in Bristol and London."

I sigh and stretch on my stool as much as space will allow. He has crossed a barrier now and deserves immediate correction, but instead a very different sentiment escapes my lips. "Yes, they do," I say.

A wisp of salt breath curls around us. *We are nowhere*, it sighs. *Time insulates your thoughts and deeds — one week, two, three before you see land again.* The feminine dream,

Eliza Egret, sprouts soft down upon her cheek, takes a squarer jaw, a broader shoulder. Something moves below my belt.

"And here I am," Bartholomew says, opening his arms as though making an offering, "against my own will, a thorn despoiling all your plans. I am the criminal you could not tame, whose return will undoubtedly cause them to question your authority!"

The young man seems sincere. His eyes, though still dog-like in servility, now convey the kind of warmth I would so like to kindle and nurture. Yet how many witnesses attested to his crimes, pilfering stores and finally setting a torch to our only promising grain crop?

"I hardly think so, young man. For your information, the Company's rules are explicit. Capital crimes must be dealt with in England. I will not be judged ill for merely following instructions."

A frown furrows his young brow, and he gives me a nod and a faint smile.

"For your sake, dear sir, I pray it may be so."

The cabin lurches in some entirely new direction — the crosswinds are particularly contrary this evening — and a succession of distant planks bark in protest. A fresh gust manages to weave its way through to us, lifting his hair and cooling my own face.

I must be mad indeed to be discussing the prisoner's fate with the miscreant himself. But this is an odd situation and we both know it. For a start, he is quite right. The Company will think I have been derelict when it comes to keeping discipline when I return to port with a bad apple, especially as it was I who hand-picked most of my men, including Bartholomew whose early schooling under a now bankrupt guardian makes him both literate and learned. Bartholomew's silken tongue gives me extra special pause, though I scarcely like to admit it. He and I will be the only two witnesses to his influence in the colony, and he presents himself so well.

But these are merely the details.

Here, in the middle of the Atlantic Ocean, we are engulfed in a special twilight where law and criminality are matters of strategy, rather than morals. As he continues to hold my gaze, his gentle, rather feminine smile playing on his lips, I realize this is not a courtesy call from prisoner to jailor. This is a negotiation. And while we are both taking pains to stay within our roles, I am also aware that, in terms of the ability of each to impact negatively upon the other, we are entering these talks, more or less, as equals. And, though I cringe to admit so much, something unexpected lures me into the agreement, the prickle of my hairs, a racing in my blood.

"How do you intend to defend yourself, young man?" I ask. I think of the excuses he gave me, the terror by night — an unmanly admission if ever there was one. A man should defend his own honour even unto death, not sneak off and commit crimes that necessitate his return.

But my question is mere bluster. Already my decision has been made, and I am ready for the extra comfort it will bestow.

CHAPTER TWO

Guy

March 1612

"How THRILLING IT ALL seems," Eliza says, her snow-white hands clasped before her breast, aqua-blue eyes alive in candlelight.

I wonder if she means it this time. I have been here before and I know that, however broad her smile, however breathless her voice, I'm far from landing this particular ship. Love rests easy only when the loved one delineates one's presence with light, one's absence with darkness. Like an erratic diamond, Eliza sparkles in all directions at once. Once I pass from view, I know only too well she will turn the same light upon another.

"Thrilling indeed," I mumble — distrustful mounds of air

passing between my lips. "It is a splendid country, full of rich and fertile soil and rolling green. As our settlement is forty-seven degrees from the pole, three to the south of our own dear Bristol, the climate makes it a veritable Eden of warm breezes and verdant life."

She tilts her head as though deep in happy reverie, but then her eyes widen.

"But there must be great dangers?"

"Dangers?"

Her eyelids flutter and a queasy suspicion of artifice enters my brain.

"I've heard of naked savages in such distant lands," she says. Her exhalation causes the candle before us to wobble. "And of strange, fantastic beasts who devour all those who dare to approach."

"No naked savages, dear lady. Just simple primitives willing to trade. No strange beasts. Just clean water and nature's calm reassuring breath."

I notice a dampening in her demeanour, but I'm eager to establish the virtues of the colony.

"The animals we brought — chickens, geese, pigs, goats, and lambs — all familiar to commonplace husbandry — took to the meadows and waters just as though they were back in England . . ."

I'm about to continue but see how all the anticipation has now drained from her eyes; her hands have slackened their clasp.

"Of course there are giant bears roaming the forests," I venture.

Her brightness returns and she glances between me and my companion as though to confirm this is true.

"Fearsome boars with sword-like fangs," offers Bartholomew at my elbow.

"Many strange creatures," I add, leaning toward her, edging out Bartholomew.

"With lions' fur but the faces of men!" chips in Bartholomew again.

"How wondrous!" Eliza gasps, looking not at me, but at my young companion. "And how lucky you men are for the chance to brave so much adventure!"

"Indeed," I say more dryly than I had intended. For a moment I am aware of the clicking of sewing needles from Eliza's aunt in the dim corner of the room. Mrs. Egret hasn't looked up in twenty minutes; she is either listening not at all or listening very intently indeed.

Eliza moves almost imperceptibly closer, her air conspiratorial. "I have heard there are mermaids in the waters around Newfoundland," she says. Her eyes have become jewels again and I know I cannot deny her. But just as I am struggling to find words to keep open the possibility of magic, Bartholomew beats me to it again.

"Silver fins and tails as far as the eye can see, my lady. The ocean is alive with them." I catch a gasp from Helen, the pretty, tall, dark-haired maid, who is filling my cup. She skips around me to see to Bartholomew. In the corner of my eye I notice her hand trembling as she tips the jug, and I catch a motion from Bartholomew's arm as though he thought to steady her wrist but changed his mind just before contact. Did he pass her something? I wonder. And, if so, what? Since our first visit a week ago he has been carrying on some form of dalliance with her. For me, he hastens to add when questioned. But I have yet to hear any useful information gleaned from their meetings and exchanges of notes.

Eliza smiles at Bartholomew. But this time her expression holds a touch of mischief as well as delight.

"At times," Bartholomew continues, "we could let down a basket from the side of the ship, dip it into the ocean, then pull it back onto the deck containing several sleek mermaids, their hair braided with sea pearls, necks adorned with laces made from starfish."

The maid has remained spellbound at Bartholomew's side. Eliza throws her a dark look and she scurries away.

"And what would you lusty seamen do with these magical spoils of Neptune?" There is a look in her eyes as she challenges Bartholomew — direct and inviting — that I don't like at all. I cough soberly.

"I fear young Bartholomew has daubed our experience too much with the colour of imagination."

"Oh, don't say that, Mr. Guy!"

Her smile is on me for the moment, but I can tell that the real channel of communication has been transferred. The conversation now flows not from me to Eliza, but from Eliza to Bartholomew.

Is it his comparative youth that demands special attention? I comfort myself with the notion that through some convoluted womanly path she might be demonstrating how fit she would be as a wife and mother. The thought corresponds with something I have read: that women shine not so much in the direction of the object of their affection but rather upon some other. This, I have also learned, is so her beauty can be fully appreciated by he who looks on, unfettered by the rigours of conversation. And, in the present situation, such an onlooker, of course, would be me. It is a pity, then, that she has chosen Bartholomew as her substitute. How could she know him to be so utterly different than he appears? Nevertheless, I draw some encouragement.

"Mr. Guy is a fine man and a true leader, Lady Eliza," Bartholomew says, as though reading my thoughts and cutting deftly against expectation. I see through the blur in the corner of my eye Bartholomew's arm rise as though about to descend upon my shoulders. Thankfully the young rogue thinks twice about this patronizing gesture and merely holds his hand suspended above me as though introducing this "fine man and true leader" to the world.

"Indeed he is," replies Eliza, "and lucky he is to have a lieutenant who possesses such a loquacious tongue."

Bartholomew dips his head in a mock-formal bow. Eliza's eyes glisten, and my unease begins to stir again.

"Have I told you, dear lady, of the sturdy trees we have found inland?" Against my will the voice that comes from me is like a gnarled walnut shell. It has no place amid the citrus freshness of Eliza's presence. I don't know why I should feel suddenly so aged — I have hardly ten years on her. Could it be that my mind and body have been formed by work, business, and care, and that Eliza is the gossamer of pure idleness? In any case, my subject is to demonstrate how, in time, hard work leads to opulence and finery. I must press home my suit. "We have begun the manufacture of our own casks in which to store all manner of provisions we have gathered from land and from sea. Our beasts are enclosed by stone walls and they thrive and multiply. Soon, I hope, our farms will yield as much grain as those in Devon and Wiltshire."

"Really, Mr. Guy," she replies. There is no scorn in her tone, but her expression resembles one who has just sucked upon something bitter and is trying not to betray her displeasure. "You should tell dear Papa of this. He is so interested in the commercial side of the colony."

I feel as though I've been reproved, caught in the act of passing a grubby sovereign to her under the table. My blunder exposed, I scramble for a footing. "Your father is a shrewd investor and he has chosen his venture well. Newfoundland is certainly a place of magic." I let the statement hang in the air. Her attention — serious, for once — is upon me. "We have indeed spied mermaids, dear lady Eliza, near enough to confirm the sighting, but too far to make an accurate report of the creature's full dimensions."

The sparkle doesn't exactly return, but something else does — a quiver in the lips, shyness about the eyes — something altogether more encouraging.

"You fascinate me, Mr. Guy, as does the bravery of your expedition, your being from England for more than a whole year." Her voice is soft, almost sombre. Something moves below my belt, and for the moment, at least, Bartholomew is scarcely present. "But tell me, does a distant glimpse of a mermaid compensate you for being so long from home? Do you not miss civilization?"

The rustle and clink of Mrs. Egret's knitting is the only sound in the room. I feel something momentous, a great cloud bringing either ruin or glory, gathering over my shoulders. "There is a small part of Bristol, dear Lady, which I carry with me, a place for which I will endure the vicissitudes of fate and vanquish all demons in order to ensure my own safe return. My selfless interest in this treasure has made me quite selfish, but this prize which makes me regard my own life as dear is neither earth, nor stone, nor gem."

Eliza holds my gaze and her face is a perfection of stillness. I feel a cannonball is suspended a foot above the table and about to fall with a great thundering crash. "Why, Mr. Guy," she says, her manner larger than before yet distinctly more distant, "a riddle! Do you desire me to guess its answer?"

Hesitancy creeps into the muscles of my face. I'm stuck for a reply.

"Come, young master Bartholomew, lend me the torch of your keen observation so that I may peer into the profound depths of your worthy leader."

Her eyelids flutter again, but now they are less butterflies than shields. They are still decorated with patterns of conviviality, but seem designed to ward off that which is unwelcome.

"It is a trifle, Lady Eliza. Think no more about it."

"No, Mr. Guy, I will not hear of such a thing. You have

aroused our curiosity. We must be satisfied. Is that not so, young sir?"

"Indeed," says Bartholomew. "Mr. Guy's wit is a known wonder to all. The only thing that surpasses the pleasure of one of his riddles is the joy of having its solution explained." I would like to flash him a warning glance but know Eliza would see it too.

"There you are, Mr. Guy, we have given up trying to guess. The code of good manners demands you explain yourself."

The candle flame leaps and Eliza's eyes lighten for the moment from deep aqua to bluish steel. Mrs. Egret has ceased her knitting and laid her bundle and needles aside. Though obscured in dimness, her frail form seems to tilt forward attentively.

Like an army retreating through a forest, I weave backward through my words — "neither earth, nor stone, nor gem" — and finally I light upon an evasion that may suffice.

"The air," I say with a slight cough.

"Surely not!"

"Yes, Lady, indeed. The air here in Bristol is what I most miss. The way that the woodsmoke mingles with the late blossoms of autumn and the crocuses of spring."

"But what about the warm breezes of Cupers Cove and nature's reassuring breath?"

Her smile — a blade scarcely at rest — remains on me. She doesn't blink, but now I've got her measure; I'll not crumble.

"I would merely have those virtues of the New World

transported hither, Lady Eliza, so that the expanse of the new and the beauty of the old could mingle as one. And now," I say, rising with all the dignity I can muster, "Bartholomew and I must go to your father's study and take our leave of him."

Eliza nods and directs a smile first at me, then at Bartholomew. Mrs. Egret's knitting has resumed and provides a clockwork accompaniment to her niece's inscrutable movements. Bartholomew bows twice, both times in an exaggerated manner, and I have to shoo him toward the study door.

MY EYES FIX ON the red bauble trembling from Mr. Egret's Florentine silk nightcap as the quill scratches through the silence.

"And so, Mr. Egret," I resume as patiently as I can, "I would be happy to provide any other information you might require on the progress of our venture."

"Time, Mr. Guy, time will give both of us all the answers that we need." The pen continues on its course, scratching sums and fractions the purpose of which I am now certain is quite unconnected to our mutual enterprise. "Our venture, as you put it, will either thrive or perish on its merits, and we will either gain or lose that portion of sweat and gold we have invested in it. Such is life."

My chest is beating an indignant rhythm that I am at some pains to suppress. "And yet, toil and risk, and, dare I say it, faith, are so often at the very heart of failure and success. In short, the fate of Cupers Cove is in our own hands."

For the first time, Mr. Egret raises his head in my direction. I believe I see the hint of a smile playing upon his white lips and the ghost of a twinkle in his pale eye. "You really believe so, Mr. Guy? How interesting, and how very like a young man to believe. You think that blind faith and belly fire can prize open the treasure chest of worlds unknown." He lays his quill carefully next to his paper. Although his spare, sardonic face retains hints of whimsy, there is a bitter sadness in the grooves of his cheek. "And yet, why should I caution or criticize? Such is the spirit that is indeed opening up the globe. It is upward and onward you must look. Why should you dwell on the English bones and tears mingling in the dust of foreign climes?"

"I venture to hope, Mr. Egret," I say, returning his smile, "that provided our company remains steadfast in its backing, salt fish, timber, ores as yet undiscovered, and not bones and tears may prove our legacy."

"So we all hope with you," he replies, frowning deeply. "I have scars and burdens enough from past failures, Mr. Guy. The world is discovering, to its cost, that a colonizing venture relies upon more than a successful yield of goods. It requires viability. And viability is a team of acrobats at a fair, a diamond of interconnected bodies rising all in perfect balance upon the shoulders of one strong man." His mention of the word "diamond" draws my attention to the wrought-gold pendant nestling within the cluster of its chain upon his desk. Inlaid with stones of mauve and green and studded with diamonds, this famous gift from a group of Venetian merchants is a curiously ostentatious possession for such a cautious man. It sits like a talisman, a reminder perhaps of his purpose in life — a studious accumulation of wealth at minimum risk to himself. He follows my flitting gaze, blinks and gives me a sickly smile. "Salt fish, timber, even ore will come to naught if the land will not yield enough grain to sustain your animals, if the animals will not multiply to feed the men, and the men not multiply to do all the required work. It was such a venture as yours that swallowed up my late brother, although it was the east and not the west to which he sailed." His eyes have taken on a forlorn and faraway look; I can see some vague, distant expanse in their paleness. "In confidence and determination, Mr. Guy, as you stand before me now, you are his very image." He gives a brief shake of the head, takes up his pen once more and begins to scratch more figures. "I only pray," he intones very slowly, as though reciting a particularly depressing psalm, "that you may have better luck than he."

I take a glance to the side. Bartholomew, who has been completely silent as I instructed him, gives me a bewildered stare. It shames me to make one last attempt.

"I thank you for your prayers, Mr. Egret, and I'm sorry for your family's great losses." I pause for only a moment. "But optimism is essential to the success of the colony in Cupers Cove and to its expansion throughout the Avalon and beyond. We have, as detailed already, harvested fish in great quantity as well as hardy root vegetables. We have built sturdy houses for living and storage and fine cottages beyond the centre of our settlement. We have weathered the first winter without loss of a man. And a successful grain harvest will, God willing, be next."

"Ah," he says whimsically, leaning back in his chair, "God willing!"

I ignore this and press on. "But thirty-nine men cannot create a society unaided. The Crown, I firmly believe, is hopeful, as are the majority of our stockholders." I pause again, this time to push home the most important argument. "It is expansion we need now, both of personnel, as you yourself suggest, and of investment. We need more men now while success is so easily within our grasp, and many more provisions. And men need wives."

"Wives, you say?"

"Indeed, sir," I say. "From the carpenter to the fisherman, from the labourer to the ironworker, all these men need both the comfort of a woman and the promise that their work may add security and prosperity to their line."

"This is true, of course." The words, spoken so softly, have little more substance than a breeze. He has stopped writing again and holds the quill sideways, running his fingertips along the rim of the feathers. "After the first season or two the colonizing workers must bring the spawn of hoped-for generations to come. This spawn must either embed its roots in the earth or dash itself against the rocks. How unlike their betters these men are, willing to bring their womenfolk into known danger. At least my poor brother had property and friends enough to leave his young wife behind. Even so, what a poor creature Mrs. Egret became after his death, and what a burden she remains!"

"May I say humbly, Mr. Egret," Bartholomew says, taking me by surprise, "that Mr. Guy has already outfaced danger after danger, both of pirates and outlaws, and our colony is safe and secure." He speaks in a low, courtly voice I hardly recognize and his hands hover over the merchant's table as though about to physically conjure some evidence in support of our suit. "The finest lady in England," he continues slowly, his wide sleeves skimming the surface of Mr. Egret's desk, "could accompany him next spring and remain in sure and certain hope of safety, happiness, and prosperity."

My face burns at his not-so-subtle reference to my dreams of Eliza, but I notice that as he regards my companion, Mr. Egret comes closer to a true smile than I believe I have ever seen in him. Deep lines radiate from the corners of his eyes, and I can glimpse what he may have seemed like so many years ago to Eliza's mother. "Young sir," he says, "how well you speak. Were I persuadable of such an improbability, I might be persuaded. But nature itself is random and vengeful. Shipwreck, blight, famine, and fever may hit the voyager when he least suspects. No discerning guardian would permit a lady to marry an adventurer." He returns his now hollow gaze to me. "I'm afraid, Mr. Guy, that you will find only the near-refuse of England, the homeless and nameless, will provide connubial comfort to your men. The colony might expand, but it needs to prove itself worthy of prosperity before we might venture more capital that way." Then his eyes seem to soften and a mild smile returns to his almost lipless mouth. This is the moment, my tingling fingers seem to tell me. Some crust of material comfort is about to be offered, some grudging extension of financial aid. "But there is some consolation for you, after all," he says quietly.

I try to give voice to a question, but like a man dying of thirst, my tongue fails me.

"You are a bachelor," he sighs finally. "At least you may rest assured that all the misfortunes that await you will not be shared with a wife."

The tingling sensation drains from my fingers. As Bartholomew and I had not been invited to sit, we remained standing all through the interview. Only now do I feel the increasing burden of my own weight, and like a man in heavy armour, I take a slow backward step. "Thank you, Mr. Egret, for that kind thought. I will continue to await faithfully more instructions from all my colleagues and from you in this business. I will gather, as arranged, women already betrothed to our men for the return voyage. And I will purchase, from our remaining balance, those supplies and victuals as might see us modestly through another season. But you are quite mistaken to call the future women of our colony refuse. If you yourself were to come to the dockside when the time comes, as I pray you might, you would find them pleasing and respectable. In the meantime, sir, I bid you good night."

As we take leave of the room, Bartholomew's footsteps shuffle around me, first in front then behind, giving the fleeting impression, no doubt, that we are a two-man country dance. The main chamber now deserted of Eliza and Mrs. Egret, and the lights out, we cross the stone floor for the main door which Helen flutters before us to unlatch. Her candle bobs and nearly dips out as the crisp night air swoops down to claim us.

"Good night, sirs," she whispers, her voice pregnant with something I cannot quite name — a sense of excitement, perhaps even anticipation — but the door closes behind us. I hear the dropping of a heavy latch.

A pair of crows, mere outlines against the moonlight, scuttle along the Egrets' chimney piece and each takes to the air, one following the other in a circular motion.

CHAPTER FOUR

Bartholomew

"WHY DO YOU ALWAYS take me here," asks Helen. "Can't we go inside?"

In the firelight, her cheek possesses the hue of one of the French peaches on Mr. Egret's sideboard. Her excitement, edged now with a touch of impatience, makes her even lovelier than she had been when I had slipped her the note at dinner. The story of the mermaids works with her every time, eliciting both wonder and fresh-teased roots of jealousy. I'd suggest Guy use it more often with Miss Eliza. But it's hopeless. Only a fool would try to breach Eliza Egret's fortress, surrounded though it may be by waves of flirtation and innuendo. She is firmly grounded in her own worth and means to scoop the cream and leave the rest. Only a fool did try. I almost pitied Guy in the growing silence after he had handed her a whip and tied himself to a post . . . "one part of Bristol dear lady . . ." I could hear the jangling of his cox-comb bells as he spoke.

"Do you not adore the dancing of the flames, Helen? In the new-found-land we love nothing better than to gaze before nature's hearth and tell stories to one another."

I hate open fires really, especially in this small patch of scrubland so close to the Broad Quay docks where we can hear the hubbub of sailors, the wretch of consumptives, and the rhythmic creak of the dockside gibbet. But I have nowhere else to take her, as Guy is keeping me grudgingly enough as a guest already. I don't mean to provoke him without reason. The pit before us is an old one; half of the logs are already well-charred. I added a few dry twigs but only for effect. They gave off a thick smoke that made Helen cough at first and complain that the smell would linger on her clothes and lead to questions tomorrow. But now there is only flame, she is quite spellbound and I have crept closer to her, inch by inch.

"What kind of stories?" she asks. I catch a faint hum of warmth from a shoulder almost touching mine.

"Stories of our adventures in the strange new land we have found. Stories of home and the ones we left behind."

"Why do you have to leave them behind?" she asks after a short pause.

I break a twig and fling one part into the flame. A spark rises in response, and then curls into a question mark.

"I was brought up to go into trade, like your master. But the family went bankrupt."

"Still, you seem to be landing on your feet."

"After a struggle."

"Do you see them?" she asks, her voice softening.

"Who?"

"Your family."

The gibbet post groans from the weight of its load. I remember opening my uncle's bedroom door, see again the rope slung over the beam, my uncle's white bulging eyes.

"All dead."

"Sorry," she whispers. "But you have a new world now."

"A new world without the comforts of home. You can't bring a lady to such a wild and untamed region. It's too dangerous. At night the sky itself is like crystal, the voluptuous moon four times its usual size. As the oceans roll onto the endless sands you can hear the mermaids whispering to each other on the spice-fumed air. And Mr. Guy misled your mistress about that too. No air is sweeter than that of Cupers Cove. The atmosphere is different in the far west; it hangs like vapour of honey, tinged with cinnamon and clove."

"It doesn't sound dangerous," Helen says, turning her body from the fire. Her knee bumps against mine as she faces me full on. "It sounds marvellous!"

"Would you not find it too much for your senses?"

"I scrub floors and empty chamber pots for my keep. That's too much for my senses, not the world that you describe."

I nod and throw the second length of twig into the fire. "But there is a cost, young Helen."

"Don't call me *young* Helen. I'm at least as old as you."

Her dark eyes, moist with anger, have caught the flame now. "I was schooled too, with Miss Eliza, at least for a while when we were children."

"Years and school. I'm talking of experience."

"Experience of what, exactly?" She cocks her head and frowns, and looks achingly pretty. "Why do men always talk like that? You think life is about miles traversed? Women bedded? Ale swilled? How about ovens fired, floors swept, silver polished? My broom has travelled more miles than any ship. That's experience for you!"

"Experience of drudgery, yes."

She straightens her neck and leans away from me. For a moment I think I've gone too far, and that I might have lost her.

"What exactly would you have me do to change my situation?"

I know it's meant sarcastically, but this is the opening I've been looking for.

I smile and consider for a moment.

"How did you leave your household, Helen? Are they all safely asleep? No disturbances?"

"Yes, everyone is asleep."

"Mr. Egret too?"

"Yes."

"I'm glad to hear he sleeps so soundly, and there was no commotion about the place."

"Now it is you who is talking in riddles."

I pause again and look into the flames.

"The Egret household bulges at the seams with riches. How does a woman like you polish and dust trinkets of little account to their owner, but of a value that might make the fortune of a modest man, or woman?"

"I don't know 'how,' as you put it, but I can tell you that fear of the hangman's noose keeps my fingers where they ought to be."

"Ah, but there you have it, Helen: fear. Listen for a second!"

I take hold of her wrist.

"What?"

"Just listen," I whisper.

I loosen my grip upon her wrist and let my hand fall. Her startled eyes, still searching mine, widen. A woman coughs and spits somewhere in the deepest shadows near the road. The gibbet creaks. A cold-fingered breeze creeps around us.

"It's everywhere, closing in on us. Wouldn't you prefer to skirmish with death than let it come upon you slowly, unopposed?" I feel her sigh, and know the thought is not new to her. "Experience, the only experience worth having, is about risk. I was not Mr. Guy's deputy when we set out from Minehead eighteen months ago."

"I'd say not. You couldn't have been more than sixteen years old."

"It's risk-taking that elevated me to where I am today. That's what the new world is all about. Its wonders are not for the faint-hearted."

"I'm not faint-hearted," she says, a wounded look returning. "You should know that by now. I've broken my master's curfew three times already to sit in the cold with you."

"What is the most valuable object in your master's house?" I ask her suddenly.

"Mrs. Egret, his sister-in-law," she says with a short laugh.

It's an answer I wasn't expecting. A flame ducks suddenly before leaping afresh.

"How is that?"

"More than two-thirds of the Egret fortune is in her hands. That's what Bertha, the old cook, tells me anyway."

"But Mr. Egret acts like the master."

She is silent for a moment, smiling perhaps at the satisfaction of her minor betrayal.

"That's what he wants people to believe, and after her death, of course, it will be so. But the largest part of the fortune belonged to her late husband for discoveries made on his final voyage. Mrs. Egret has the power to name her own beneficiary."

I think of Mr. Egret in his study, his thin lips, his scratching nib, a fortress of inscrutability, shielding his daughter, guarding his household. I let the image hang in the flames, then I return to my present purpose.

"Apart from Mrs. Egret, what is the most valuable possession?"

She turns away from me, staring into the fire, her hands straying upon the shins beneath her dress.

"His trunk, I imagine. It's full of any valuables he doesn't entrust to his bankers."

"Think rather of the most valuable object that is small enough to put in my pocket."

"That would be his pendant from Venice."

"The one on his desk with the diamonds, rubies, and emeralds?"

She turns to me again, a curious smile appearing on her face. "You *are* a sharp one!"

Now I dip my hand inside my pocket and, feeling the gold hot against my fingers, I draw the pendant out by the chain. Rotating slowly, its emeralds and diamonds dance in the light of the flame.

A gasp — sudden and guttural as though coming from the earth — has escaped Helen's lips. She sits now, shoulders hunched, hands over mouth, a prettified gargoyle, quite incapable of movement.

The pendant ceases to turn; like a proud courtier it merely bows, first right then left, stones winking, rubies bleeding light ominously.

"Why would you do such a mad thing?"

"To prove my point."

"You'll have us both hanged!"

"Not if you return it before your master wakes tomorrow."

"Never!"

"Why not?"

"I'll not take it even for a second."

"That's most unfortunate." I open my free hand and let the pendant sink onto my palm, the chain gathering in a mound as I lower it. "You see, if they find it missing, they'll know it's you. Only the maid has access when the master is not in the room. He didn't see me take it. I know that."

"I'll just tell them it was you."

"Then it's my word against yours, which is not good for you. I can talk my way out of most anything and . . ." I send her a look of pity which is, in part, at least, quite genuine, ". . . honest folk like you do have a way of giving themselves away even when they are almost entirely innocent."

"What do you mean 'almost entirely'? I had nothing to do with this!"

"No, but you snuck out at night for an assignation. They will smell the smoke and you'll have grass stains on your dress. Believe me, Helen, once a woman compromises herself as you have done, men will believe anything bad about them."

She lets out a sob and gathers the front of her dress in her fists. "You must be the Devil. Did you plan all this from the start?"

"I don't plan at all," I tell her plainly, "I merely prepare and see how matters unfold. There are limitless possibilities in any given situation. It's a mistake to fix yourself too rigidly to any one course."

She is breathing hard, still fixed on her knees before the fire. I weigh the pendant in my hand. "What shall I do with this, then?"

She looks across at me, face streaming with reddened tears.

I make to throw it into the fire.

"No!" she says, leaping before me with surprising swiftness. Her fingers wrap around the chain.

"You'll take it back?"

"Do I have a choice?"

I think about it for a moment — really I do; I suspect she thinks this pause is part of my cruelty, part of the act, but the core of me is more honest than people know — "No, not really," I say.

Then, gathering the chain and pendant, she gives me *that* look — eyes narrowed, venom tears — that I knew would come from her sometime. I just didn't think it would be this soon.

"So just tell me," she asks, her voice surprisingly mild considering the circumstances, "is this it? You watched me at the table, passed me notes, met me in secret, just to find a way to implicate me in your crime. Now I go home, try to return the pendant without being caught, try to avoid slipping my head into a noose, while you bide your time and then return to new-found-land?"

"No, my Helen, not at all." I take hold of her free hand which is moist with sweat and tears. She does not pull away at first. "This is just the beginning. I ask if you can take risks and you have proven that you can. Now we are partners. Now we take all our risks together."

She withdraws her hand gently from mine and wipes a sleeve across her face. Looking at me askance for a moment, she balances on her heels and starts to rise. I stand with her.

"I've got to go now and deal with this," she says, as though the obvious might be in doubt. She buries the pendant awkwardly up the same sleeve which had received my love note and she fixes me once more in the light of the now dying fire. "You had better be worth the trouble."

She turns and walks away, weaving like a ghost between the fires of frozen revellers and vagrants, until her figure merges into the night. *You had better be worth the trouble,* she said, and the words seem to echo in the darkness, sending odd tingles from my legs all the way to my scalp. I feel I may have met my match.

CHAPTER FIVE

Helen

Not for the first time since meeting Bartholomew, I can't sleep. Moonlight skims across the room, settling on Bertha's bed in the corner. The rolling contours of her blanket, rising and falling with each of her snores, seem to map a continent of mystery and magic. The darkened valleys pulsate with unknown life — unicorns, two-headed lions, rivers of nymphs and sea horses. The luminous snow-topped mountain peaks hide underground caves full of crystal ice inlaid with rare stones.

My world is spinning in wonder. My toes itch to accomplish some unnamed quest. With his red lips and his clear blue eyes, Bartholomew seemed so young, so fresh when we spoke together for the first time only a week ago. But since then I have found his certainty of manner, his impressive bearing and confidence, gives him a strange kind of wisdom which draws me toward him as the moon draws the tide. I cursed him tonight when he claimed me as a co-conspirator and thief, especially as he had coaxed my employer's secrets from me first — although, if truth be told, I'm embarrassed at how little coaxing I needed. Then, as I made my way back to the house, as I slid in through the same parlour window through which I had made my exit, taking up the study key from its high nail, and shuffling moth-like into Mr. Egret's study, my heart hammered with something greater than fear: I was in the process of discovering some great truth about myself. The possession of riches, whether acquired by means fair or foul, *is* exhilarating. Danger is exhilarating. Returning the pendant was a choice and this made me, for the moment, a queen, especially because I knew how easily it could be taken again. I saw the pendant to its place on the desk, not gasping in terror, not ducking shadows as I might have supposed I would, but quietly, comfortably, daring the darkness to uncover my crime. I stroked the chain, taking my time and even polishing the gems with my sleeve.

The world is changed now. Stars reel in confusion. Rivers change course or flow upstream. The air I breathe is scented with some new hope, and the poor frightened maid who, at least in part, feigned tears to Bartholomew by the fire is no more. She, my drab cocoon, is cracking and peeling away. My master, Mr. Egret, recedes in my imagination and becomes no longer the whole of my life's landscape, but the frail, hunched man that he is. His outlines are distinct. There is delineation and limit to his powers. I hear the whoosh of his cane and feel the smart pain my mother must have felt when, in a fit of temper ten years ago, he struck her. Was it the shock of this attack that brought on her final illness? Bertha had once hinted this was the case.

I think of the months of her decline, how I slipped into her shoes as she wasted away, and sank, like her, gradually into the shadow of Mr. Egret's giant vulture wing. I feel again the hiss of Miss Eliza's venom, the tug of her fingers in the roots of my hair as she transferred the whole of her anger effortlessly from my mother to me. I would no longer be schooled with her. Now I was only a maid and I must not forget it.

For the first time all this does not seem part of some natural course ordained by the movement of the stars, but rather pure chance, subject to alteration. I can't imagine lifting another mop or scouring another pan, although I suppose I must for the time at least. Fear of the noose, the stocks, and the prison cell has shackled me to such tasks, but I have been an ant stuck in the rock crevice of custom and example, unaware of the vast expanse of land which lies beyond. It is such folly to hold one's breath, and remain silent and still in the hope that death will not notice us. Better to engage in the struggle for life. Better to chance the consequences. If the new world is opening up to fresh and infinite possibilities, then so can I.

CHAPTER SIX

Guy

THE WIND BLOWS LIKE Armageddon, lashing the sails and spiralling around the crow's nest. The wave ridges sizzle as the white foam mounts higher and higher against the hull. I wonder if it's the tempest only that creates a constant clamour of voices — women's voices — yelling, whispering, laughing. A silver tail emerges and disappears just as quickly into the foam, and a sweet, oozing sensation comes over me as the hope rises that this might be Eliza in mermaid form.

Bartholomew appears before me, his feet anchored firmly against the tipping deck, though I am shunted back and forth and have to grasp hard to the deck rail. He gives a bow, mock-polite.

"Looks as though we might sink, Mr. Guy," he says, smiling.

I try to answer, but the wind swallows the words and I

am not sure myself what I am trying to say. When Bartholomew speaks again his voice is impervious to the elements, strong and confident.

"With no money, few provisions, and poor soil I didn't think we ever had much of a chance," he says.

I don't answer. I know that if I try to put my own exasperated fury into words they will be stolen again. The deck tips violently and I am almost wrenched from the rail, but my wet fingers just manage to hold. Then I am tipped in the opposite direction and the force of it buckles my legs. My ribs are flung hard against the rail. I scuttle like a dancer to get my footing.

"It's very simple, Mr. Guy," says Bartholomew, still perfectly relaxed. "The whole project was bound to fail. You brought females for the goats, females for the cock, females for the sheep, but no females for the men." He points over the side, to the mountains of heaving, bulging foam whose peaks now reach almost to the deck. "And this is what happens to the imagination of men who are cooped up together too long."

Another tail appears, its ribbed flesh glistening and wet, and wriggles above the foam before disappearing. The voices grow louder and sweeter too, like a merging of hitherto incompatible sounds — a high pealing bell the softest of whispers. The creature appears again, this time headfirst, golden hair, like Eliza's, crowning her head then separating into thick strands running down her long white neck and shoulders, her smooth back and — as the mermaid arcs farther from the water — along her middle region where skin turns green and puckers into scales.

I catch her gaze just as her head disappears into the foam, the perfect curve of her body following. Her smiling eyes, I noted, are aqua-blue like Eliza's; her red slightly open lips formed a smile. Together with her nakedness and with her joyful abandonment to the clinging foam, she has reversed the perpetual question mark that hangs teasingly over Eliza. The creaking floodgates are swinging open at last to a *yes*.

Though the swaying deck conspires with my own weight against me, I climb, swinging one leg over the rail, hauling myself over, feet touching down on the outer deck rim. I watch the bubbles bulge, catching rainbow swirls of colour, before they pop and disappear. I steady myself briefly, and then jump.

Immediately honeycomb sweetness rises to my embrace and my whole body tingles with gushing warmth. The mermaid Eliza whispers and wraps her wet hair around my skin and I feel as though I am lost in an eternity of pleasure. Bartholomew yells at me over the deck rail something about a dream.

I try to ignore him, but his voice persists. Though still gliding within the substance of pure pleasure there is something flat and motionless beneath me. I find that balance — or lack of balance — has gained in importance suddenly, and that the soles of my shoes are struggling to find a firm surface upon which to stand.

"Mr. Guy," he calls again. I peer from just beneath the surface of the foam and see him indistinct, a candle in his hand. How could a candle burn so steadily in a tempest? I wonder. "Mr. Guy, are you ill?" He is closer now, walking on the foam perhaps?

The room is dark, only the faint bronze hue of candlelight warming the walls. The ship is gone, as is the foam, and the sea, and Eliza the mermaid. Bartholomew is standing halfway between the doorway and me. I am in bed. Raising my arm to my mouth, I wipe my lips dry with the cuff of my nightshirt.

"How long have you been there?" I ask.

"Ever since I heard you calling out. You must have been having a nightmare."

"I was merely dreaming. I am quite well." I haul myself up against the pillow. It has been some time since he has joined me under the sheets. A faint desire mingles with my loneliness, but I know it would unman me to yield to that surrogate passion to which all seamen cling. There is no excuse now. Eliza herself is within reach. "Where have you been for the last two days?"

He pauses, one of those distrustful silences, enough time for such a mind to weave any tale it pleases.

"Come now, answer quickly!"

"I had to meet someone after our dinner at the Egret house."

"Who?"

"A young lady."

"Who, I say?"

"Helen, the Egrets' maid."

"Her again," I say with a touch of relief I daren't examine.

He shrugs and a smile ghosts across his face.

"Just remember our bargain, Bartholomew. You are working for me. I won't save you from the gallows a second time."

The smile intensifies. I have invoked a past that his mocking air likes to deny. But I won't let him deny it. He would be dead now if not for my mercy.

"I *am* working for you, Mr. Guy. That is why I had to meet her and why I had to follow up on certain paths she unwittingly opened to me."

"Then why didn't you apprise me of your plans?"

The candle wavers and shadows duck over his young face.

"You would have slowed me down with your questions."

"Well, here's a question, you young rogue: what use is the information of a maid when it is her master we are trying to influence?"

He turns and gestures at the stool at the foot of my bed. I nod. He draws it into a clear space in the middle of the room and sits, laying the candle and holder on the floor.

"With respect, Mr. Guy, only a man who has never been a servant would ask that question. A servant is key-holder of the household. A servant knows where the family's riches are hidden. And like the creaking floorboard, a servant knows all their secrets too."

"How would this help us? We need support from Mr. Egret. We are neither robbers nor blackmailers." My voice fills the room like a whiplash, as though Bartholomew and his secret — and there must *be* a secret for him to talk as he does — were twin lions I am at pains to keep at bay. But why should I be afraid of any secret? skips the question across my mind. Is it because I am afraid of the uses to which my ambition might put it?

Since Bartholomew disappeared, I have been roaming the streets of Bristol by day and the darker streets of imagination by night. Every twisting thought, every weaving plan was studded by noose, scaffold, and stocks. Nothing within the law, nothing within the narrow confines of morality, shed any sunlight upon my desires. Why, I wonder, would any man ally himself with someone as fearless and immoral as Bartholomew unless he intended to heed the advice of the damned?

Bartholomew pauses before answering. With the light below him, Bartholomew's face seems almost angelic, like the visage looming from a fresco inside an Italian cathedral. "I am searching for weaknesses and for alliances, that is all. Helen is already ours. I am certain she will act in any way I instruct her."

Curiosity burning my ears, I fling off my bedclothes and stand. "I am seeking an honourable approach," I tell him, pulling my breeches on under my nightshirt, "an honest and straightforward argument which may persuade Mr. Egret to venture more capital and to persuade his friends to do the same."

I catch Bartholomew's eye and don't like what I see; it's an expression close to pity. "How is that tactic working so far?" he asks softly.

I snap up the belt from the trunk in the corner and fasten

it around my waist, my face heating with indignation. What *does* he know? How can I get him to tell me without asking?

"Mr. Egret will risk no more than he has to," he ventures. "He has told us as much already."

"It is in the nature of business to keep a closed purse until proof is provided of a lucrative return. He must be persuaded."

"Or compelled."

I take a step nearer. Anger rather than curiosity might bore the information out of him. I want to learn his devious alternative, all right, but I mustn't lower myself so far as to seem interested.

We are almost exactly the same height, and the way he meets my eye has always that mild yet fearless quality. He never flinches, nor backs away, and I feel his confidence draining mine before he even begins to speak.

"You are quite right," he says in clear, virtuous tones. "An advantage obtained through underhanded means must be disregarded and forgotten, even if it is the difference between certain failure and certain success."

He bows, takes a step backward and turns to leave the room.

Only as he reaches the doorway does my tongue come unstuck. "Just one second," comes the order in a strange high-pitched voice. He turns again, a look of amusement playing under the surface of his expression. "Just out of interest only, just so I may know more of your tactics, my boy, what is this secret that you believe yourself to have uncovered?"

"Oh, nothing really." He shrugs, making to go once more.

"Come, lad, tell me."

He returns to me like a cat, furtive and coiled.

"It is only this: you are making your pleas to the wrong man and your loves to the wrong woman."

"Explain yourself!"

"Mrs. Egret," he says softly, "the creature in the corner with the knitting; it's she who holds the purse strings you wish to loosen. The poor brother for whom you heard the old man mourning — it's his interests which have brought old Egret his gold. But he is merely the heir to his brother's widow." He smiles at me now. "Opens possibilities, wouldn't you say?"

"How so?" I snap back, and I can feel that moral shell that neither Bartholomew nor I believe in becoming harder but more brittle. The beast of ambition within me growls, sensing prey in Mrs. Egret. "Assuming your information is correct, there's a fortress around the old woman. Who can get to her but through her brother-in-law?"

"Mr. Guy," he says. "Are we not adventurers and explorers? Is it not our vocation to go into regions with hazards and dangers and re-emerge with our prize?"

"We are in Bristol now, boy," I tell him. "Bristol requires neither astrolabe nor charts, but honest and straightforward business."

"Humbly, Mr. Guy, I might mention I have observed that even here in Bristol, as in every other place on earth, business is seldom either straightforward or honest."

For a moment I am lost for words. This time, it seems, it is really quite obvious he has a point.

"What would you have us do then, Bartholomew?"

"For two nights and a day I have been working on this."

"Working?"

"Searching among the forgotten corners of the shire for a key that might open Mrs. Egret's memory and stir her to generosity."

He's trying to wait me out, his face calm and impassive.

Impatience gets the better of me: ". . . And?"

"I have found him. He is waiting downstairs."

CHAPTER SEVEN

Bartholomew

Like the most awkward of six-legged creatures, the three of us make our huddled way in silence through the lightly falling snow. Mr. Whip stops frequently to gather his breath. His meagre elbows need supporting by Guy on one side, and I on the other. By the time we reach the Egrets' door, I am afraid the powdery snow gathering around our feet will make the old man slip before a meeting is achieved.

Keeping one hand under Mr. Whip's elbow, I go to knock, but Guy motions me away, raises the iron knocker with a flourish and lets it fall once, twice, three times. He sends a white funnel of breath through the air and I can tell he is uneasy.

The door opens, quickly revealing Helen's face oddly flushed beneath her white bonnet. Her eyes briefly take in the group but rest on me. They darken in the centre in a way that is rather pleasing.

Guy gives a cough.

"Tell your mistress, *Mrs.* Egret, we have a visitor for her."

The order is sharply delivered and Helen's lips pucker a little, her eyes narrowing. But she turns back to me and I nod. She retreats and motions us inside. With some jostling and a brief lifting motion, we ease Mr. Whip over the threshold.

"The master is in church with Miss Eliza, but his sister-in-law is here."

It seems like more information than is needed. We can clearly see that Mrs. Egret is in the corner of the spacious room, in the very same seat which she occupied two nights before, knitting as she did then. But Helen's words are for me. We have Mrs. Egret to ourselves. It is the opportunity for which I was hoping.

The old man is the first to shuffle forward, his feet moving far more quickly than before. The four sovereigns of Guy's that I handed over to him jangle in his purse as he closes on her. Guy and I follow him, one on each side. Dimly, the old lady's head rises from her work. The needles tap against each other twice and then stop.

"Matilda!" exclaims Mr. Whip, the three syllables collapsing upon themselves like the constituent parts of a cartwheel rim breaking under a heavy load. His angular frame stoops toward her like a storm-ravaged bird spying its half-forgotten nest.

The old lady's filmy eyes try to focus. Her mouth opens

slowly, and the knitting drops first from her lap to the chair, then from the chair to the floor.

"Philip?" she whispers.

Mr. Whip nods slowly. A tear now runs down his hollow cheek.

Mrs. Egret leans forward, her swollen fingers gripping the arms of the chair. "Philip?" she asks again.

"At your service, madam."

His hands descend shakily into her lap. Hers rise from the chair rim to meet them.

"The years," she merely says, "the years."

"Yes, indeed."

Helen slips a stool beneath the place where she imagines the old gentleman will sit, facing Mrs. Egret, though he shows no signs of wanting to rest now.

Backing away slowly, I reach across and tug at Guy's sleeve. He wrenches his arm away and glares at me, but still follows me grudgingly to the exit. As I take Helen to the side, Guy rather awkwardly addresses Mr. Whip. "We shall return in twenty minutes to convey you to the carriage that will take you home, sir." Neither Mr. Whip nor Mrs. Egret paying him the slightest attention, he turns stiffly on his heel and leaves through the main door, motioning me to follow.

I take Helen's hand, turn it palm upward and, passing my own hand over hers, let Guy's sovereign drop. Her smile at my touch turns to surprise as she feels the gold. When she looks into her palm, displeasure floods her face.

"Does money insult you, my Helen?" I ask, taking pains to ensure there is kindness in my challenge.

"Other things please me more, sir. Like honesty and trust."

"Is gold the enemy of honesty and trust?"

She is rolling the coin in her hand now, adjusting to the feel of it, her expression betraying some struggle.

I must follow Mr. Guy. My fingers touch hers once more and then I leave through the still-open door.

Guy is scowling at the empty street as I alight.

"Two sovereigns for the maid, and eight for the old man," Guy says testily. "An expensive scheme, my lad, at ten pounds; it had better work."

"It will, Mr. Guy. We must reunite Mrs. Egret with her past, remind her of her intrepid husband, and make her associate his memory not with her brother-in-law but with us. You know it takes money to win people over and ensure they act in our best interests."

Guy turns and surveys the falling snow with some sourness.

"I may be a dull man," he says under his breath but loud enough for me to hear, "but I have always been hard-working and decent."

He turns to me and I find myself looking away, though I am naturally anything but shy. My face burns too, and I sense now a glint in his eyes as he recognizes the unwanted nature of his confidence. "Yes, hard-working and decent. I dislike tricks, my young friend."

His glare remains on me and finally I'm obliged to look at him. He says nothing else, merely holds my stare, but I understand the reproach: *and this is what I have come to.*

It's odd, this sense of responsibility that sweeps upon me

like an unexpected wind. I am the nephew of a merchant fallen into insolvency, an orphan turned apprentice cook, turned convict, turned imposter. How came it about that I should wield so much power?

I remember the paths that met at a rough crossroads on the hill above Cupers Cove, how the stubble of wheat and barley, freed of the weight of bulging kernels, skimmed against one another in the breeze, reminding me that the shed below was crammed with enough winter food for our beasts. The constant double blow of hammer and echo, hammer and echo, came from below as men laboured like ants over the new twelve-ton boat. Escape was on my mind, but the colony's apparent success was my prison. I had approached Guy once, and saw the flex of impatience about his jaw when I mentioned the roving eyes and hands of his men. His words were like the heavy fastening of a bolt: "There are no articles to cover such occurrences. You are a man. Defend yourself."

I prayed for deliverance instead, following by rote the murmured verses of my childhood, adding the desperate heat of my shame. But there was no God here. We had either tipped over the horizon beyond His sight, or He was simply unheeding to begin with. Action, I decided, was more potent than faith. As a cook, I always carried the means to induce flame: a cloth, a flint, and some powder. My fingers tingled and rooted in my pocket as the thoughtless breeze swept around me once more. A distant cumulus bulged over the sea, heavy but retreating. If God would not help me, I thought, I will conjure a devil that might.

CHAPTER EIGHT

Matilda

I SENSED SOMETHING WOULD happen this morning even before I heard the three loud knocks, before Helen scurried to the door and admitted the visitors. Ever since I awoke and returned to my habitual corner, portents have echoed in the click of my needles, in the breeze-like rustling of my wool. Within the bulging folds of new cloth which grew upon my lap, I saw the rise and dip of unknown mountain ranges.

Sundays are always quiet, but this silence was so intense I could hear the thump of my heart and the creak of my joints. So when he came toward me, this man, nimble and upright for his age, when his shining eyes claimed my attention, his name — *Philip Whip* — passed through me like a ghost before I could have reason to hope it might be him.

And now we are alone. Like the stirring of soft wings within the hard, dry casing of a caterpillar's home, life is returning. The mean, grey years are falling from me. The dust has been so thick and so stifling that at first the memories were too blinding to be endured. Only through the kindness of the handsome face before me can I be guided safely back into the light, to memories of my Nicholas. I trust Philip's clear, blue eyes as a blind woman might trust a soft and comforting voice.

"Have you been in Bristol all this time?" I ask him.

"Some miles distant in the country, my Lady, I have dwelt a quiet existence this fifteen years past, though in my dreams I venture still to the blue seas of the Mediterranean, to the wild frozen wastes of the north, to the deserts of the east where I travelled once with your worthy husband."

"Ah," I gasp, feeling the affection of his phrases close too tightly upon my heart. "You and he were men indeed, men indeed." His hand comes down upon mine again and I hold back further tears.

"Why did you not come to see me all this time?" I ask with more reproach than I intended.

"I did, my dear Mrs. Egret, twice soon after I purchased my house in the country. Both times your brother-in-law sent me away before I could see you. He told me you were too sick to be disturbed and I should not come again."

A band of heat stings my forehead as though I had been struck with a lash. I am used to seeing my bother-in-law's dry inadequacy as neutral — a blind, unmoving barrier against joy; I have never before thought of it as a *predatory* greyness, an invading dust which harms wilfully and with malice. He sees my reaction and smiles.

"He may justly have thought me a vagrant, the first time anyway. I was still recovering from my final travels, tired, sunburned, and disinclined to dress for company. He perhaps considered me a likely carrier of some foreign plague."

Grief heaves inside me again. Despite my old friend's kindly interpretation of his behaviour, I have a sudden vision of my brother-in-law as a wingless vulture sitting on the threshold of the mean house, pecking and harrying the most exotic of migratory birds, one of which carried messages of friendship and of love lost. Who else might he have turned away?

I am aware that a wealthy widow is never more than a few steps from the ducking stool, the scaffold, and accusations of witchcraft. My own riches have remained a firmly concealed secret, and my brother-in-law's status in the community has always cast a deep shadow, obscuring me from Bristol's scavengers. I have no surviving family but he and Eliza, and it is true Mr. Egret, the younger, has been my protector as well as my jailor. Like oil and water the incompatible elements of anger and thankfulness swirl inside me. "If I have been sick," I say at last, my voice weak, "it is a sickness brought on by want of those I have once known who are now gone from me. He had no right to turn you away."

"But I am here now," he says, his smile widening, "thanks to the two young rogues who brought me. What do you think of them, my dear? The pretty boy bribed me to come to Bristol again, can you believe that? Four sovereigns to see my old comrade's honoured wife and my own dear friend?"

His smile is infectious and I find myself excusing what is surely inexcusable. "He *paid* you?"

He nods again, chuckling. "Does it not remind you of Nick and me? Remember the way we used to bribe your father's servants to gain entrance into your household? Once, do you recall, we mistook your rich uncle as a servant and passed him a coin, which, I remember he took with a smile."

I make to swat him away in jest. "You two were young fools!"

"And yet was not this same spirit that put wind into our sails, that prized open the world and its riches?" As though to illustrate his words, a gust finds its way unexpectedly into the room and I find the passageways to my lungs filling with freshness. I see Philip and Nick as young men with packs and donkeys making their way through yellow sands, to the land of spices and adventure. For a moment I'm too full to answer him.

"Now," he continues, "merchants grow rich with fleets under sail, a thousand scribes and accountants at their bidding, and the banner of the East India Company to give bluster to their canvas. But it was young fools such as Nick and I who paved the way."

I look into his face again, his eyes the pure blue crystal of understanding, framed by the deep granite of hardship, travel, and time.

"Why did those young men bring you to me, Philip?"

"To plead their case, I imagine, my dear."

"How would they know I possess anything worth pleading for?" I ask. I feel suddenly like a fresh fallen car-

cass in a meadow; I sense the circling shadows of birds over-
head.

"Matilda, the true adventurer call smell gold from a
thousand miles, so you should know they are genuine when
they converge upon you rather than your brother-in-law. In
any case, I hardly needed persuading to see you. In bringing
me here they have taken me back to my youth!"

He holds my hand again and I feel layered years of
boredom, heartache, and frustration peeling away, exposing
me to the harsh glare of the sun and to a terrible pain as
urgent and fresh as the day it was first felt.

"And you will leave me neither as I was, nor as I am, dear
Philip, but a spirit stretched and tortured between those two
opposite poles." I want to add that part of myself died upon
that eastern mountain slope along with my Nick all those
years ago, and that when Philip himself brought me the
news months later, then disappeared once more into his
seemingly eternal voyage, that the rest of me disappeared
with him, that the dry husk that remained seemed worthless. But what can adventurers know of the women who are
left behind? What can they know of love if safety is their
concern for us? No one's mind and body is really designed
to await news of others in danger, except perhaps poor Eliza,
the butterfly under glass. Eliza, whose energies have long
been warped into a sabre of spite, particularly to those who
threaten to claim her father's attention; she is perhaps the
kind of creature imagined by Philip and Nick. But she was
raised by her father and knows no other life. Though young,
Eliza is already my counterpart in futility and lifelessness.

Like a good maid, Helen has sensed her presence might be needed and has presented herself before us. "Tell the two young men outside I will see them now."

As I watch Helen curtsy, back away, then move swiftly to the front door, I have the strange impression that Philip and I are like ancient gods viewing from a distance the shadows of the people we once were. I sensed butterfly hints of flirtation last night between Helen and the good-looking boy, and feel that the magic of Nicholas, Philip, and I must have risen like vapour during our youth to hang in the air until this moment and then fall afresh, enriching these young people, causing them to sprout fresh shoots of love and adventure.

The two men return on the heels of the blushing Helen, Guy first, then the younger one, lighter of step than his chief, almost dancing in eagerness as he steals glimpses of Philip and me over Guy's shoulder. My incongruous sense of power as they halt before me and survey my expression for clues makes me feel as a small dog might if suddenly presented with sceptre, crown, and bowing courtiers. What *shall* I decide? I have no idea. Indignation rises at the thought of my brother-in-law, gatekeeper against my will. But the gratitude of the sheltered and tired clings upon the shards of my anger like moulded lead upon the edges of stained glass.

"So, young men," I begin, "what is it that you would ask of me?"

The older looks to the younger for a moment as if for guidance. Then he coughs and straightens his shoulders. He holds his hat before himself rather in the manner of a penitent before a shrine.

"Gracious Lady, you may have heard of our travels and our labours already."

"In great detail, sir. I was in this very room last night when you described them."

He seems to colour for a moment. I have perhaps reminded him of his doomed attempt to make love to my niece. Then he stands even more erect, comically formal. "Our great efforts to make our dear colony successful rely upon the faith and support of those who reside at home."

The younger man frowns and casts his eyes to the floor.

"The backing that we have, the financial backing, is limited . . ." he falters, his wary eyes skipping along the tapestry above my head, to the Egret coat of arms, a scrawny carrion bird in whose talons resides a sword. "The original stock is curtailed to such a degree that profit may be stifled . . ." The younger man steps forward suddenly, startling Guy though his voice was already beginning to trail into silence.

"My Lady, if I may," says the handsome youth. He gestures to his companion as though about to prove this rather dull creature an example of particular fineness of character. "You must understand this great man has a burden upon his shoulders as heavy as the greatest explorers known to history. Great Julius himself, travelling from Rome, could scarcely have felt the eyes of future generations as keenly as Mr. Guy does today. He seeks to bring the glory of civilization, godliness, and culture to the astounding but desolate beauty of Newfoundland. As Rome was to England then,

England is to this new territory now. It is a satellite of ourselves, my Lady, and a legacy we dare not neglect. We are bringing all that is brave and steadfast into the dark and untamed wilderness. It is nothing less than a holy mission."

His words dance in the air like flames of pure mischief. I look into his intelligent eyes. The unrestrained, mellifluous tone of his voice brings him as close to my ideal of man as anything I have heard since the time of my dear Nicholas.

"Young man," I say, smiling, "it seems you imagine the old to be lured by that which is holy, just as the young are to be tempted by mermaids and pearls."

He takes a step closer, a smile — knowing and flirtatious — upon his face now. "It is the wildness of adventure that makes it holy. When the spring comes we will throw ourselves upon the fierce crosswinds of fate once more. We will seek danger and glory afresh, and we trust, dear Lady, you will give us your blessing and encouragement."

"*Only* my blessing and encouragement? Well, young man, you have those already."

His smile remains on mine and he doesn't blink. His companion is as red as a fresh-scrubbed radish, and his feet shuffle in a distracting manner.

"I see it is something rather more that you seek," I say, returning his smile. "You have reunited me with a dear friend, it is true, and, in courtesy at least, I must promise you something in return." I pause, realizing that the conviction of my words belies an infinite uncertainty. I wonder if this youth has actually shamed me into the valour of decisiveness. It feels that this is so, but how? As the room turns slowly and I try to root my senses, I realize he has so successfully evoked the spirit of my late husband that in refusing him I would be dishonouring Nicholas. I look to the elder of the two men. It is he to whom any pledge must be made. "I cannot, in conscience, disinherit my brother-in-law while he lives," I continue, rather shocked at myself for putting such an idea into words, "nor can I punish my niece. But if he should die before Eliza turns twenty in a year and a half hence, she will need a male protector. My brother-in-law should have dealt with this possibility a long time ago, but he is a man who clings to life and will not think of the possibility of the long and dreamless sleep that naturally awaits us all." The acrid sting of disloyalty dries my tongue, but I press on.

"Should Mr. Egret die in the next eighteen months, he will leave one woman old and declining, another under the age of legal inheritance. The avaricious neighbour and the witchfinder both will prick their ears to the possibilities." I pause for a moment.

Mr. Guy stares at me, his lips silently mouthing the words I have just spoken as though in an attempt to understand their meaning. I look from him to his companion. The younger man's face is alive with calculation.

"I will bestow upon you, Mr. Guy, the honour of being Eliza's protector in his place should Mr. Egret's life not span that eighteen-month bridge to Eliza's safe inheritance. There is no other family upon which I may rely. You will, until that time, have at your disposal all my wealth and all the interest which you may use at your discretion. You will, no doubt, continue in your bid to win her. And if you do, my fortune will be yours in perpetuity."

"We will need a notary, my Lady," says Mr. Guy's companion quietly.

"You may call on the judge next door," I answer. "You have perhaps fifteen minutes left before my brother-in-law returns."

The younger man bows and takes a backward step. Guy follows suit, confusion still twisting his expression. They leave. As Helen has slipped from the room also, Philip and I now sit in silence. The room is perfectly still. It must be fancy, the tiredness of my vision, but a soft blue smoke lifts around our shoulders and a burning has entered my nose. A moment more and the illusion passes.

When they were young, Philip and Nick used to practice hitting targets with their pistols. I remember the smell of gunpowder, and the way that the smoke moved like a cloud. I thought then how easy it would be, too easy perhaps, to take aim and lay one's finger upon a trigger, how death might follow the merest twitch of thought.

The words of my pledge run through my mind once more, and I see again the earnest understanding in the younger man's eyes. I know I will not rescind the promise; it is my repayment to love and valour and is as sacred as a vow to the dead. Yet, dimly, the knowledge grows that something beyond my control has been set into motion.

CHAPTER NINE

Guy

"SHE MEANT WHAT SHE said and nothing more," I insist again. "There is no call for reading into events more than exists, my lad."

Time and time again during the last few days, since the strange meeting between Mr. Whip and Mrs. Egret, since the lady's proposal that followed and the amendment of her will, Bartholomew has returned like a pesky wasp to the same dead point — *what does she really intend us to do?*

The tavern door opens again and a rush of freezing air scatters some of the sawdust from the table between us. "Only a fool would find encouragement in anything she said."

Bartholomew catches my eye, says nothing, and takes another gulp.

"What?" I demand.

"Sir?" he says, mock-innocent.

"What do you mean by that silence?"

"Silence, Mr. Guy, usually signifies an absence of meaning."

"Not with you."

"If you want my opinion, sir, I am more than willing to give it."

He raises his tankard. His clear blue eyes fix upon mine over its rim.

"Then give it."

Bartholomew lays down his drink.

"The old lady has issued a challenge," he says, eyes lowered, one finger tracing a pattern in the table's sawdust.

"So you keep implying."

"She has told us of the obstacle her conscience forbids her from removing. At the same time she has cleared a path for us to profit by the removal of that same obstacle."

"It sounds like a riddle, boy."

His finger, which has created a full circle in the sawdust, stops. "Rather an easy one to solve, wouldn't you say? She cannot remove the obstacle. She is asking us to do it for her."

"What would you have me do?" In spite of the bitterness of the ale and the sourness gathering in my mouth, I take another swift gulp. My stomach jumps.

"Sir, I would merely have you do all that your ambition and desire deems necessary."

Ambition and desire — the words glow hot in my belly and I have a queasy sensation that Bartholomew is merely giving voice to my own thoughts which, too timid to form themselves into words, have remained in a dusty swirl of confusion. Within hours of our meeting with Mrs. Egret, I did recognize such a challenge. Even as she spoke those words "if he should die," the vision of a bloody knife circled in my brain. Only when we had dealt with the notary and emerged from the dimness of the house into the clear winter's day, did the idea of violence firmly consign itself to the world of nightmares. And there has been some comfort in resignation.

Ambition and desire are terrible things, much more punishing than defeat. Ambition and desire respond to hopes whether they are godly white or criminal black. They never rest.

Before Mrs. Egret's "help," I was just becoming used to the idea of failure. The early promise of the colony — the noble effort it represented — was already beginning to replace ambitions for success and expansion. My near-miss was already becoming my gleaming city upon a hill, a dream always receding, always out of reach. It had, if truth be told, already become the "almost" of my career, the country of my founding that never quite was. A laudable effort which is thwarted possesses a comfort, and a pristine, unsullied quality that no victory in the world can ever match.

And then there is Eliza. Eliza is the name whispered in my blood as it courses through the channels of my veins. Eliza is the word mumbled by my heart as it thumps its way through the dreamless night. How glorious it was beginning to seem to live a whole life under the golden shadow of unrequited love! How delicious indeed when I now consider the alternative of the stark, dangerous action that may result in the acquiring of all ambition, and the end of dreaming. Eliza, the dream, is worth any risk, but can the same be true of Eliza the woman? It is a paradox. The risk I am considering is the one thing that might win her as a prize and turn her from Eliza the dream to Eliza the woman. Would such a victory merely break the spell?

As I begin to answer Bartholomew, I feel like a man with outstretched fingertips reaching timorously into a dark and unknown space. "My ambition and desire," I say quietly, "do not require the breaking of the sacred, moral codes passed down to us all and learned by rote in the schoolroom." I wonder at the weakness of the statement, the placing of myself in the position of a child. Am I begging him to persuade me? Or am I pleading for a way to excuse myself from the obvious course of action?

Something like a smile, but more subtle, calculated, and intelligent than any I have seen on his or any other face, takes possession of his features. "Moral codes are themselves subject to perpetual change. In times of stability and opulence, compassion and charity reign supreme. In times of danger, the sword of valour is sharpened. Qualities rise. Qualities fall. My dear sir," he says, lowering his voice to a whisper and edging across the table. "Until fate dispossessed me, I too learned by rote the lessons of history and morals. Humble though I am, I did learn this much: When the scribes and scholars come to review the history of the world, they will find there is only one consistent virtue. That virtue is success."

PAUL BUTLER

I move back in my seat, a mannerism designed to mag-
nify my distaste. My ale is almost drained and a new thirst
has already begun. The barman is filling a jug, I notice, and
will be at our bench before long. "You sound like the worst
kind of skeptic, young man," I tell him. "One who denies the
existence of human good must surely deny God also."

"Whose god?" he asks in a whisper. "We are colonizers,
Mr. Guy. Our God cannot afford to be faint-hearted."

I feel like the traveller who, having stumbled upon the
wrong path, sees no alternative but to keep going. If only I
had handed Bartholomew over to the authorities as I had
originally planned before leaving the colony. If only I had
not unchained him on the ship, or at least confined him
where he could not roam. If only Bartholomew had not persuaded me to bring the old adventurer, Whip, to Mrs. Egret.
These and so many more are missed chances for a safe
return to modest ambition, or no ambition at all. Now it is
too late. Night is drawing in. Our destination can only be
arrived at through the most deadly of perils, physical and
moral. I have given this young jester the power to influence
others as well as myself. I have allowed myself to be
tempted, and the temptation is such that only the most self-
defeating cowardice could induce me not to yield. If I falter
now, my whole life will be rendered void of meaning. To
others I might become the man who almost colonized the
eastern portion of Newfoundland. To myself I would become
the man who saw a chance and closed his eyes until it was
over. I would have chosen failure over success and would
thoroughly deserve the lack of attention given to me by

Eliza, her mean-spirited father, and even Mrs. Egret and the old man. How right the young man before me is to invoke the heretics' argument about the changeability of virtue. All I really know about Bartholomew is that he is a liar and a thief. Yet everybody looks upon him with favour. His charm is undoubtedly his wildness, the fact he is quite unfettered by morality.

The barman arrives and I nod. His foul beer comes in a torrent, sloshing and foaming to the top of my tankard. He fills my companion's mug also and leaves. The Crossroads Tavern has always been a place of hard business. Despite the extra security of hushed voices, the people here know not to listen in.

"Well, young man," I say, mustering as much authority as I can, "let us put our words upon the table. If you yourself were in my position, how would you proceed?"

CHAPTER TEN

Bartholomew

IN THE RISING WARMTH of the night, the snow has melted and seeped into my shoes. I gaze up at the dark outline of the Egret roof and wish I could get as drunk tonight as Guy was when I saw him home. His gloom-laden words and maudlin self-pity weigh upon me now — *you think me a dull, heavy-footed man, don't you, Bartholomew? You think I'd turn a poor jig at the fair, a fellow who lacks charisma, no doubt? You're all laughing at me, you twinkling-eyed youths with your pretty faces . . . your mermaids . . . and your serving girls. You're all in it together, I know* — But the words that came before this final descent into incoherence irk me most deeply: *how would you proceed?* I felt as though he was breathing his own ambitions into me and setting me, his personal devil, loose to fulfill them.

Am I fated to forever be the living embodiment of temptation? I envy Guy that he is able to thrust his present thoughts and future sins upon another. I was his mirror and, like all moral cowards, he cursed his own reflection, calling me a godless skeptic. Of course, he agreed upon the act of murder which has no doubt been nudging him ever since the notary witnessed Mrs. Egret's altered will.

The simple switch of responsibility for the crime established, he outlined a way I would profit, becoming one of the stockholders. The trap — his, though no doubt he believes it is mine — was complete in a matter of minutes. He wanted no details and would merely await the accomplishment of the task.

The rain beats its paws against my face and the same spray farther afield — tiny arrowheads arcing toward the ground — catches the distant starlight. The dark window immediately below the steeple under the roof must be Helen's room. An emotion has come upon me that is quite new and, in a sense, frightening. It makes me want to take root in the ground upon which I stand and hunker down with another who might comfort me.

I know why I'm weak. Guy's gasping stupor brought Cupers Cove to me more vividly than I would like. Since leaving him the ghosts of that time have been on my heels: the gimlet-eyed men, the creaking floorboards, the hot breath upon the back of my neck. Ever since Cupers Cove I have been burdened with a cloak of grime.

The mermaid sightings were always a prelude to trouble; the word itself, mer-maid, became a double toll, a warning of the unwelcome stirrings that the night would inevitably bring — shuffling movements amid the snores and belches, the sliding, surreptitious approach while with eyes closed I would try to count how many were converging upon my bunk. And once, the final time before — in desperation — I burned the grain, the pitiful whisper in my ear, a plea agonizing in its abject brutality. "You think you're something, don't you, Bartholomew?" These were the logic-free words that formed themselves inside the man's hot gasps while my neck hairs bristled like ripening corn. "You think you're better than us?" The weight of his trembling hand was upon my arm and I recognized the shameful, clodhopping request for love, with envy and violence substituting for tenderness.

My crime with the grain freed me from all that, at least for the while. But I knew there would be a cost and even sensed that, like interest upon a debt, this price might be subtle and rapidly multiplying. Guy unshackled me on the homeward voyage and even raised my stature in Bristol, but now he has turned me into the arrow of his desire and the receptacle of his guilt. I may be godless, but I do not mean to gamble my soul on the mere hope it may be worthless. Like a good investor, I will share the risk. Like Guy, I need a proxy.

Bald ivy trails like rope up the Egret wall. One tendril creeps its way toward Helen's window and I am filled suddenly with a sense of the daring and dramatic. The feeling seems appropriate enough. As an adventurer I am, after all, selling the notion of danger. And I know enough of risk to suspect that, like crime, it can be infectious.

CHAPTER ELEVEN

Helen

THE BIRD SCUTTLES ALONG the window ledge again, this time pecking at the glass. I turn from the sound, drawing the blanket around me, shivering not so much from the ice splinters reaching through the walls as from the prickle of wool. I am in some unknown darkness between the opposite extremes of terror and excitement. But, then again, are they opposites? Like the two contrary directions of a hoop, they seem to emerge as one and the same. The flame inside me teases *every* fear and expectation. I can hardly tell pleasure from pain, fear from anticipation.

No one made clear the relevance of the visits several days ago, least of all Bartholomew. But I know that the sudden shift of Mr. Guy's interest from Mr. Egret to his late brother's wife, the visits from the old gentlemen and the judge who acts as the family notary, surely all point to the information I gave to Bartholomew that night in front of the dockside fire. All these things could only mark some change in financial fortunes. Should I be in fear of the stocks for betraying my master's confidence? I hear the whoosh of his cane once more; feel the stab of the metal against my mother's skull. It is this one brutish act together with its likely consequences that stand out when I think of him now. I even remember more details of the occurrence long darkened by memory. I hear again my mother's whispers behind Mr. Egret's half-closed bedroom door, and feel the creak of the stair upon which I crouched. Like swooping butterfly nets my ears managed to catch from my mother's lips two hushed names, "Mr. Egret" and "my Helen," both in pleading tones.

Then, like a rolling wave, a phrase from Mr. Egret tumbled into a hiss: "Remember your place!" There was a shriek and then a sob, and the collapse of knee upon floorboard. I rushed in to find her crouched upon the rug, tears of blood dropping into her cupped hands.

Why the change? Why the return of memory? No lasting grudge accompanied me all these years from girlhood to the present. The assault merely faded into a rumour, a whispered confidence from Bertha. If I retained any resentment in this home it was against the hair-tugging Eliza. And even this faded when Eliza's childish spark crusted into distaste. Once I was out of the schoolroom, and no longer shaming her slowness in learning, I was scarcely a threat.

Am I kneading the past until it takes the shape and texture that most justifies my betrayal of him? Mr. Egret's sudden loss of temper, his blow, is the only thing that fits such a purpose. There are other aspects to his character. He did keep my mother under his roof when, husbandless, she became round with a babe. Most masters would have turned such women from their door.

I shift again, wool scratching my chin. Remorse is surely beside the point when the hammer of the law might at any hour of the night beat its way through to my bed at dawn and drag me screaming through the mob. As if in premonition of such an event the bird scratches at the window again, this time with unusual persistence. I wonder if fear, as well as guilt, is distorting my vision. Perhaps there will merely be more of the same: creaking silence while the foundation of the house continues to settle to a new reality. There has been no commotion at all since Mr. Whip's visit. I heard none but the most routine of conversations between Mr. Egret and his sister-in-law. Today there was the silent roast lamb at one o'clock, Mr. Egret's afternoon retreat to his study at two, his gruel and bread at five, his bed at eight, and now the same untroubled snoring from Bertha. Surely if things are terribly wrong under this roof, it would seem so. But nothing has changed. Does Mr. Egret know about the visits and simply not care? Or will he remain in the dark until the next visit from his banker, which could come on any day? Will the house suddenly explode into uproar?

I simply do not know enough about the dealings of the world to make a decent guess, although I do know that nothing is more important than property and that no purse can ever be threatened without exciting the most extreme of passions. It is difficult then to imagine how a catastrophe of some sort can be avoided.

I have never entered the circle of women and men who look upon money as more than bread, milk, and oats for today and tomorrow. Food and shelter are the only currency I know. But I can see the feverish activity behind Bartholomew's upward climb to riches and I understand the significance well enough. He is thinking not of today or tomorrow, but next month, next year; an old age in safety and opulence; a life without labour. Perhaps there are nobler yearnings too: a wife and family, a growing tribe. Of course a colonial boy would have to think that way; he is forging a new limb of history.

I am breathless at the thought and my face stings with heat. In the vision of his family that skipped through my mind, I realize, the hair that curled under the bonnet of Bartholomew's pretty wife was black, like mine; her eyes, though indistinct, were brown, also like my own. The vision is not only noble in its way, but exciting.

Still, something in me recoils from the baseness of money. The sovereign he dropped into my hand was a shock greater even than his theft of the pendant. That trinket merely had to be replaced. Bartholomew's sovereign, however, was a different matter. The boy clearly believed he had purchased a piece of information from me, a slice of intelligence that I had no right either to possess or to give. The moment I felt the gold upon my skin, I heard the turning of a heavy lock. I had taken and passed to another someone else's secret. I could give back the payment it had earned, but I could not undo the crime.

Yet even as I imagined the hammering of prison shackles upon my wrists, something other than fear was sparked. It was another kind of token I had wanted from Bartholomew, not the golden kind. Even in disappointment I carried on searching my palm for some message beyond the crude metal, and then I lifted my gaze to scan his face. Was I searching for a softness there that might belie the ugliness of the transaction?

I did find something, a word not said but thought, perhaps even passed between us; I was his *accomplice*. Was there not a strange intimacy in the word? Better than "partners," the term he had employed by the dockside fire. *Accomplice* is soft and clandestine, the sound of lovers collapsing into a hollow, the hushed folding of limbs, the whisper of infinite trust. Each crossing of our paths — the slipping of notes at dinner, the dropping of a coin in my palm — had the silken texture of true understanding. We were in it together, even though I hadn't any sense of where the journey was taking me.

The bird knocks upon the pane so hard, I turn upon the bed and raise my head. There's another thump as I steady myself on an elbow and try to peer through the misted glass. Something is pressed up against the pane. I have seen wood pigeons fighting over a mate, and the grey object that rises and falls against the smearing glass seems like a wing at first. But then I perceive some larger bulk, a twisted branch perhaps, of which the object making contact is only part. Only it makes no sense as there are no trees on this side of the house. Startled now, and drawing comfort by Bertha's steady outward whistle, I swing my legs and let my feet touch the cool wooden floor.

Wrapping my nightshirt snugly around me, I pad toward the window. A step or two from the pane, I stop, breath suspended, ears numbed. A hand, fingers white, bloated against the glass, appears from darkness. My first thought is that a nightmare has spilled its banks, a breach occurring in the wall between waking and sleep, and that all manner of phantasms will soon tumble into the world — men with beaks and feathers, disembodied hands, seaweed monsters and skeleton armies — unthinkable horrors which have so far been made palatable to men and women only by the swift dissolving forgetfulness we associate with dreams.

The window frame judders and I catch the outline of a face looking through the glass; something cracks, and there's a shimmer of dry leaves, then a thump far below. Whatever was up there has fallen, I realize, but the face and form remain with me with their suggestion of thick wavy hair and a tapered chin. It was surely Bartholomew. No thought at all imposes itself between this realization and my blind descent on the curling stone staircase. As I daren't light a candle I feel my way down the wall as an insect feels with probing hairs, my thoughts all the while dancing over calculations of falling — three storeys: twenty feet, thirty — and juggling visions — Bartholomew with a broken shoulder, a broken wrist; Bartholomew dead.

My bare feet pad along the carpet and stone to the front door and, very carefully, I turn the horseshoe lock. The door gulps open to a rain-streaked night and Bartholomew stands before me, a trail of dead ivy on his head, but otherwise apparently alive and well, a pained, imploring look upon his face.

"THIS IS NOT A decent place," I tell him, liking neither my words nor the hint of a whine in my tone. "The Crossroads has a reputation. You should not have brought me here."

"This is a private room, Helen, not a regular part of the tavern," he replies, a soft, feather-like quality in his voice. "It isn't used by other patrons. My cloak covered your entry and will shield you from any eyes upon your leaving."

Of course this is true enough. No one is around and, even if they were, they would catch hardly a glimpse.

I know that whatever strange alliance we seem to have formed, we lie far beyond any consideration of what is or isn't seemly. To speak to him as lovers in courtship speak would be to miss the point somehow. It would be taking something brave and new and trying to mould it into an object of uniform drabness. Still, it's an effort not to be like this. Beneath his cloak that still drips despite the tongues of fire that leap behind the grate, I am in a nightgown only. Beneath the nightgown I am naked. Under the table the bare soles of my feet skim ridges of sawdust. A nudging voice, my poor dead mother, tells me a tavern is not a place for a decent girl no matter the hour, and it's now close to midnight.

A dry fold of his cloak, warmed by the fire, touches my neck as though to encourage me, to prickle me into the reality of the comforts I may claim. Bartholomew is strangely silent, his brow furrowed, his fingers tracing patterns in the sawdust on the table before him.

"Why did you risk yourself in so foolish a way tonight?" I ask gently.

"I had to see you." He looks up at me now, his eyes startling in their blueness.

"Why not wait until morning?"

A sad smile passes over his face.

"Because you, like me, are a servant. You own nothing of your life, least of all your time."

"So you bring me another sleepless night. Thank you."

"Have you had many since we met?" His eyes glisten, sad yet playful.

I pause for a second. "Yes," I say, "many." I feel the sudden lightness of an unburdening.

He smiles. "We must meet sometime, Helen, and are only we free to do so when our masters sleep."

I weigh the idea for a moment. Everything he says is pleasing, the implication that our fates are joined, the suggestion that we are equal in servitude and that we must then understand each other with the minimum of explanation. But I've been here before, and know that comfort can flip like a coin into trickery.

"You are hardly a servant," I tell him. "You are Mr. Guy's deputy."

"Not exactly, Helen," he says, raising his tankard to his lips, sipping and lowering it slowly. His eyes are all the while on me, and strangely intense. "Guy's deputy is a man named William Colston. He is in Cupers Cove still."

"But you are not a servant," I pursue. "Not like me."

"No, not like you," he says. "I am beneath all servants, Helen. The rope around my neck ensures that. I must do Guy's bidding no matter how foul the task."

There is heat and bitterness in his face now.

"Why? What rope?"

His head merely shakes in answer as though shrugging off a fly, and his gaze returns to the tankard before him.

"Lies," he says, "just lies. But the false witness of a gentleman is worth more than the truth on the lips of a thousand peasants. Guy is wielding the accusation over me. This is why he has me follow him around in the guise of a friend, and attend the feasts to which he is invited. I am the eyes that covert on his behalf, the ears that eavesdrop at his command, and the hands that steal at his pleasure. I am a wretched, miserable slave, my Helen."

"What about Mr. Egret's pendant? How was that theft committed on his behalf?"

He is surprised by the question, I can tell. His body lurches sideways as though avoiding a knife throw.

"For once I decided to use the skills gained under his command, but for a different purpose. I had to, Helen." His hand jumps across the table to mine, and I feel the warmth of his fingers. His eyes search my face, almost pleading now. "I had to be sure of you. I had to know that you had the courage."

"Courage for what?" I tug my hand back, but not strongly enough to break contact. "Don't trick me again, Bartholomew."

He holds my gaze for a moment and he is close enough for me to feel his breath upon my face. He seems like a man in turmoil, but with Bartholomew I have learned to distrust my own judgment.

"On my life," he says slowly, drawing out the words as though they were stones that pained him to disgorge, "I swear. No more tricks. I knew you were the one the moment I saw you. I knew the path we could both travel together in life, but only if I could shake this noose from around my neck, only if I could break Guy's shackles. And he has promised me freedom and more, wealth and position enough to bring up a family free from penury and threat of prison. Can you imagine that, Helen: the two of us making our own way in the world? There is just one final task I must perform. And I need your help."

"What task?" I ask. It is not the answer to this question that I need. I am more than willing to help him. What I need is proof of his sincerity. "Tell me how this may be achieved!"

CHAPTER TWELVE

Bartholomew

THE FIRE BURNS LOW now. The residue of ash shows white like powdered snow against the iron bars of the grate. Helen's fury still burns like a comet through my mind, but there is something blessed in the smoke.

I stoop and throw a fresh log upon the sunken mountain range whose peaks are the last ridges of sawn wood and whose river valleys are slow-cooling dust.

I had to try. I had to push the boundaries of success as far as they would go, and a small part of me is still disappointed; it would have been so simple and clean with Helen as an ally. But mostly there is relief beyond any I have felt since November last, when the homeward sail bulged and the masts creaked and the course was set for home. Helen will not be my murderer. I must find another course, slower and more tortuous. It is the curse of my ambition that I must seek for that which I would rather have refused to me.

Beyond my horizon lives a man of riches and endless pleasure. He is impatient for me to reach him, and his is the voice I must listen to first. My future self knows not only wealth, but security. He commands judges, and armies obey his will. He nags and harries me. He allows me no peace until his destination is achieved.

A swift assassination and a share in the Company's fortunes would set me on the road. But the gorge of Helen's non-co-operation has been met. I have no choice but to skirt by its perimeter. Months, perhaps years, have been added to my journey, as well as dangers and hazards as yet unknown. But it is a wholesome feeling still, the sting of her refusal.

"Do you like Mr. Egret?" I asked her, the flames dancing to my words.

"He is my master," she shrugged. "I never think of like or dislike."

"Is the world a sweeter place for his presence?"

She laughed in reply — a mirthless, nervous laugh — and when her features settled again, I thought I saw signs of lingering bitterness.

"It's a simple choice we have been given, Helen. You, more than any of us, are in a position to deliver results."

Her face, dark eyes alive in firelight, returned to a vision of confused innocence.

"What choice? What results?" she said. "He is alive. You cannot profit unless misfortune falls upon him."

The trick now was to remain completely still and let her

words hang. A frown slowly creased her pale forehead. Her eyes narrowed into a kind of questioning, then a plea, and her head tilted like that of a dog which tries to comprehend an alien sound.

"The choice, Helen," I said softly, "is to languish in slavery or to act and take fortune in our hands."

"You can't mean it!" she whispered, hands now rising in a girlish steeple to her mouth.

"This is how the world is," I said, reaching my hand to her, palm resting just above her knee.

"Murder," she said, eyes now rimmed with red. She hardly noticed my touch, so my hand remained, gathering heat.

"Far more common than you think, Helen."

Her knee shifted, perhaps without my knowledge, so I let my hand remain.

"It's the language of politics, Helen, a well-trodden route to advancement." I shook my head and fell upon my knees like a man out of his mind. "I am as terrified of this as you, believe me!"

She gaped at me, hands slowly slipping from her mouth, an expression I couldn't name — could it be sadness, even pity? — upon her face. I had aimed my arrow with care; when all else failed, I reasoned, vulnerability was surely the one quality no woman could resist. I had a hand upon each knee now and my fingers were pulling folds of her night-dress into my palms.

"It is fate that has brought us here, Helen, not careless ambition or cruelty. Are we such fools that we imagine we can live happily without stealing another's air? Do we not tread upon many ants and spiders when we make our way through the market? Do we not drown a dozen ticks when we plunge into the river? All effort has a cost, my Helen. We cannot make our bed without cutting straw."

Then it all happened. Her fingers burrowed under both of my wrists, shifting my hands from her legs then letting go. She stood slowly and, when she spoke, her voice was somewhere between a whisper and a hiss. "Villain, I am not *your* Helen!" The expression that had confused me, I now realized, was neither sadness nor pity. The water in her eyes would surely have scalded had I touched it. "You have already turned me into a thief and informer. Now you would have me commit murder." She gained the door before I could stop her, but turned a final time. "Oh, Bartholomew," she said with a shake of her head. The tear running down one cheek now, together with the unexpected use of my name, suddenly touched me quite deeply, and I was rendered mute. "You are a worthless young man!"

And with those words she was gone from the room, footsteps descending the staircase, the side door shrugging open then banging closed.

IT'S CURIOUS WHAT MORSELS may encourage a man. While individually the words — *villain, worthless* — seem to damn me in her eyes, there is something in their context and organization that gives me hope. Tears are not shed for a villain. Women do not brave the night for the worthless. Nor do they allow the touch of his hands to linger. I think not of her refusal to submit to the task, but of how very close she came. And now, as the room begins to warm and tiredness creeps upon me again, I thank whatever stars reign over Helen's thoughts and movements tonight that she did remain firm. There is no end to ambition's duty but that which virtue imposes. I cannot find virtue in myself, so my ambition would have remained quite unchecked but for Helen. Helen's virtue, then, has allowed me a moment of rest.

Closing my eyes I allow the hiss and crackle of the now-growing fire to wash over me like a reddening stream. The Crossroads does not close and it seems as well to drowse here as to return to Guy's house and endure his pitiful cries and tortured dreams.

A noise comes from far beneath me — two short coughs perhaps — and I think of Cupers Cove, with its storms, its hail, its bone-gnawing cold, its half-finished buildings, with unfastened doors of slippery pine banging through the endless nights. I see myself as I was there, a figure unrooted, drenched in foreign rain, soaked in the stealthy secret vices of my displaced countrymen. Unresolved questions thump to the memory of the wind: how to eliminate Egret; how to keep Guy's favour; how to profit from the Newfoundland Company; how to profit but avoid returning; how to return but avoid attack. Footsteps — approaching footsteps — have merged into the rhythm and I realize the initial double cough was not a cough at all but the opening and the shutting of the Tavern's side door, an unwelcome realization now as the door and staircase lead to this room and I really don't want to carouse. Reluctantly, I stir myself to take leave as the newcomer reaches the top of the staircase and the door opens.

The hooded figure before me neither speaks nor shows his face, but his shoulders, slim and youthful, make the stranger very close to my own size. Steam swirls upward from the fabric of his coat, and rain drips from its hem. The coat's colour — purple grey — and the stitch, fine and flawless but for a single frayed thread hanging in a loop from the arm, announce the garment undoubtedly as my own.

I stand suddenly, chair scuffing backward along the floor. This can't be a dream. The senses are too precisely etched and coloured for such a hope. But I find myself scurrying after the impossible, as mice must scurry from a house on fire.

"Your coat," comes a voice from within — a voice without expression. Its tones, unmistakably feminine, nevertheless ease my terror in a stroke.

"My coat," I gasp, my heart still pounding, my ears hissing as though with a chorus of snakes.

"I had to give it back."

"Of course," I say hoarsely. "I had forgotten."

She lets the hood drop at last. With her dark hair wet and in some disarray, Helen looks like the handsomest of crows. Illogically, given her words, she moves toward the chair she had vacated earlier and, far from handing me the garment, only draws it closer around her shoulders as she sits.

I sit also, pulling my chair forward. My knees still quiver

from the shock and my heart skips wildly. Though abating, my first wave of fear has given way to another anxiety, less urgent but no less serious.

"It could have waited," I say. "How long have you been outside? You left more than an hour ago." My voice is high-pitched and words fire rapidly.

"Does it matter?" she answers, looking not at me, or even at the wall behind my head but at some unseeable distance.

"To me, Helen, yes it does. I want you safe from the elements."

Her eyes turn upon mine.

"Is that true?"

"Yes."

"Is it?"

There remains something trance-like about her, though her attention is locked upon me now.

"Yes," I repeat. "Why are you here, Helen?"

The hissing subsides and my ears go rather numb as though suddenly afraid of what they might hear.

It is through movement of her lips rather than through sound that I catch her answer: "I've changed my mind," she says. "I'll do it."

CHAPTER THIRTEEN

Helen

I'VE SAID IT, AND now my words are his. I can't reclaim them. But he doesn't seem delighted at all. Instead there is a mask-like fixedness to his expression. He looks rather pale and his eyes will not settle on me for more than an instant. Is it my imagination or do his lips even tremble as he speaks?

"You'll do it?" he asks like a frightened boy.

A vow, even if spoken in haste, is safe enough if the recipient doesn't mean to exploit it. This is how I feel now. My willingness to act has landed not upon the stone where commandments are etched. It has landed in a nest of feathers. Reluctance, not gratitude, has greeted my promise to spill blood. Suddenly *I'm* the one who feels stained by murderous thoughts.

"That's what you wanted," I tell him, impatience, and perhaps a little panic, creeping like an army of spiders over the skin of my shoulders. I couldn't have mistaken it all, could I? He couldn't have meant something else? The word "murder" never actually left his lips. It was myself only who gave it utterance just before I left him and ran in a state of fury and indignation into the night. And now with the words "I'll do it" I have completed the noose of guilt, eased it carefully over my head, and handed him the end of the rope.

MY CHANGE OF MIND came with the crushing of a snail shell.

I had run from the tavern, bare feet scattering wet pebbles from the Broad Quay into the water, mast bell mocking me through the dark. Arriving at my master's house — the place of my mother's life, the place of my own birth — I had begun circling the building over and over. Why could I not enter, climb into my customary bunk, and forget about the hand at the window, Bartholomew's fall, and my own so easily won night journey to the Crossroads Tavern? Why could I not shed the young man's horrible plan along with his dripping coat and get the sleep that would enable me to resume my duties refreshed?

I felt the sharp stab once more as Mr. Egret's cane whooshed through the air. This time, the imaginary blow seemed to dig deeper, right into the bone. In this reliving, the girl on the stair was aware of something vicious and unjust, aware also of anger already burning in her belly even as she listened for the oncoming shriek, the sob and the collapse of knee upon floorboard.

Yet he was kind enough most of the time, wasn't he? He let my mother stay in his employ when she was with child, let me scurry under the feet of the household. In the early years he allowed me to learn my lessons alongside Eliza with hardly a division of rank. Later, after Mother died, he would come upon Bertha nurturing me into the ways of service, and would nod calmly, give me a thin smile and even a pat on the head.

But why was he so charitable to us? The question hung as I watched the rain fall. Each droplet carried a fragment of the moon and slowed to half its speed when I caught and followed its movement. Mr. Egret was not renowned for his generosity of spirit, and my mother's life was a catalogue of regulation — not established in rueful guilt but through long and tireless observance. A tavern, she told me, is not a place for a decent girl no matter the hour. The warning in her eye held neither suspicion of me, nor remorse for herself. It was merely a fact, known and adhered to. My mother did not go to taverns, ever. Her name — Isabelle — rang through the tiny community of shopkeepers, widows, and barrow boys like a chime spelling good sense and restraint. A glance from her was enough to silence horseplay and have the roughest of boys touch his hand to his cap. How did this strict and disciplined woman with no suitor come to be with child?

The answer was like a pattern in the wood, obvious but unimportant. The knots and swirls had always spelled a face — two narrow eyes, a bent nose, and thin mouth — but the rag that cleaned had barely time to care. What passion would cause a cautious man like Mr. Egret to strike a servant after so many years? Why would the servant care enough to wither and die?

I watched a raindrop disappear into the earth, walked a little farther and felt the crack of the shell as it splintered beneath my bare heel. Bartholomew's words returned — *do we not tread upon ants and spiders when we make our way through the market?* Here I was already a murderer and all I had done was tread upon the ground. Raising my foot, I heard a multiple crack as the shell fragments fell upon themselves. *Inevitable*, was the word that sounded in my ears, a term of fragile constancy. Everything crumbles. Mr. Egret would certainly die one way. Ten years, or five, or three would be too late for some.

But what had it to do with me? I continued circling the house, my feet scratching against the pebbles, the rain seeping at last through Bartholomew's coat. I thought of my mother, betrayed by his secrecy; I thought of myself obscured by his shadow; I thought of Mrs. Egret, her late husband, Mr. Guy, and Bartholomew, each of them journeying to unknown shores, risking themselves for every gain. Mr. Egret seemed like some giant carrion bird which preys not upon the dead but upon the living.

I reached the spot where I had crushed the snail. The ridges of its shell fragments caught the moon. *Inevitable*, the jagged edges seemed to spell. The reins of all knowledge — Bartholomew's plan, Mr. Guy's hope, my mother's death, and my likely paternity — had all been drawn together and placed neatly in my hand, and as fate, or providence, would have it, I also had easiest access to the target. Why should he live to thwart so many?

"YES, YES," HE SAYS, rising, shuffling around the table, shoulders oddly stooped. "It's the course we must take." He picks up a log from the pile, though the fire is burning warmly enough, and hurls it over the grate. The new log dislodges one already burning, sending a swirl of sparks into the room. The glowing underbelly of the upturned log fades into grey. Slowly, as I watch in silence, the first timorous tongues of new flame tease their way around the base of the fresh wood.

"How?" I ask his back.

His feet and shoulders do not move, but his head flicks in my direction. I can see his high cheekbone, the tip of his nose.

"*Atropa belladonna,*" he mumbles, and then turns. I've heard the phrase before. It tumbles from the mouth like a snatch from a love sonnet, caressing and smooth. He stares at me now, his face a mask, drawn and unmoving.

"What?" My question comes out like a cough.

"Deadly nightshade."

The voluptuous phrase dissolves, falling in soft leaves to reveal a blade.

"A poison?"

He nods and then comes to the table. He sits close to me again, body hunched, elbows on knees, hands over his mouth as though preparing to catch whatever words might be spoken. "We must plan carefully," he says. I'm surprised at the whiteness of his face and at a slight tremor of his fingertips as they stroke his light, boyish beard. "I will collect it, of course. You must make sure it finds its way into his food."

The chain of guilt is oddly comforting. I imagined the plunge of a knife, the drop of an ax blade. This way the murder is shared. Who is more responsible: the supplier or the one who applies the poison? I was readying myself for the title. *Murderess!* — the word hurtled through my brain as I saw the sea of shaking fists, and the stones hailing down upon my head. Now I can apply a prefix: *semi-murderess!* Which mob could squeeze vengeance into such a cumbersome chant? Only half of my soul will be damned. Hellfire will last only half an eternity.

His right hand falls from his young beard and comes to rest upon my knee. Is the brain behind those distracted blue eyes aware of it? Does he know his fingers are working at my nightdress for the second time tonight, gathering fabric as before, then dropping those same folds, then beginning afresh? It's curious, this compulsive, repetitive action. I can feel his breath on my face, but it seems to contain the heat of agitation, not of lust. I sense that for the moment I am an extension of him. My leg, my nightdress is of no more consequence than the beard that he smoothed with those fingers.

"When?" My voice is sharp, urgent to rouse him. I shift my knee. His hand drops without protest.

"When," he repeats like a distant echo.

"I don't want to wait. The crime will grow larger and larger until the moment it's committed."

"Yes," he whispers like a man emerging from a dream. "We must overtake remorse before it swells and forbids action." His eyes, rather bloodshot and tired, meet mine now, and I see the tensing of his jaw as he raises himself in his chair. "We must act," he says.

My stomach suddenly churns and certain knowledge descends. The wheel is already turning; the operation to which he refers will not be commenced next week or even tomorrow, but now.

CHAPTER FOURTEEN

Guy

How did Eliza come to be in my bed? The question surfaces again, but I push it down until it sinks under and Eliza's soft, white arm emerges from the folds of linen. Her skin, unaccountably wet, hisses as it slides against the sheets. Ridges of foam appear and disappear with every movement, and the taste of salt comes and goes in my mouth.

The sweetness of it all is almost beyond bearing. Any more pleasure would surely tilt into pain. Still, I am worried. What about her reputation? Bartholomew, the young rogue, comes freely into my chamber whenever he pleases. The thought of Eliza sullied by smirks and whispers distracts me. The ebb and flow of her movements, though delightful to me now, would be branded in scarlet shame if revealed to the light of day.

For the second time I try to tell her.

"Eliza . . ."

And for the second time her forefinger presses my lips closed. She holds me with her smile, teeth dazzling white, eyes defying the dark by catching pools of fire from no source at all. Her face plunges into my neck and sweet breath rises to my earlobe.

"No words," she whispers.

But I can't help trying to speak, although I give up the idea of voicing anxiety.

"I can't believe it," I say.

My eyes, opening once more, catch the wriggle of her tail as it disappears beneath the sheet ripples.

"Nor should you," she whispers, her head rising and falling close to my other ear. "I am merely your dream."

I laugh at the idea as her tongue touches the hollow beneath my lobe. I know dreams. They can't enliven all the senses at once, elevate the spirits to heaven for so sustained a period. This plane of existence is more real than any I have ever lived through. If there is a portal to another world, then it is that other world, not this one, which is a dream.

"Sure, it's true," she says, her breath now dancing across my forehead in search for fresh zones of pleasure. "I cannot be real because you've done nothing to deserve me. If you let others take your risks, you must expect others to gather your rewards."

My eyes open again and I see people in a horseshoe circle around the bed — Bartholomew, the dark-haired Helen, Mrs. Egret, Mr. Whip leaning on a stick, and even Mr. Egret — all gazing at our writhing bodies, faces impassive.

"Rewards," I repeat. Her face travels down my chest now, her tongue marking each rib, lips touching like the warmest of summer rains. The moisture from her skin drips upon me now and the sweetness of the fluid intensifies the tremors already overtaking my flesh.

"Rewards," she repeats. Her breath gushes hot down my body. Thunder growls in my ear and rumbles down my spine and legs and across my arms. Everything flexes at once, every muscle and bone, every finger and hair, the bedposts, the walls, the shutters hiding the window. My blurred vision scans the expressionless faces gazing down upon me. In unison each of them breaks into laughter. Hands are thrown together in mad applause: Mr. Whip ignores the stick that clatters to the floor as he beats his palms in celebration; Bartholomew, jumping madly, strikes his hands together over his head; the maid dances a jig around him; Mr. Egret nods and cries like some bird for its mate. The noise is tumultuous, like a playhouse crammed to the rafters. My legs kick against my will like a man condemned after the stool is pushed from under his feet.

A second wave follows — clapping, cheers, foot-stamping — in power diminished from the first. It comes a third time but, like a flapping wing of a storm-threatened crow, the sound is muffled and ceases too soon. Finally each of the spectators is still. Mr. Whip groans and falls to the ground. Helen yawns and sags at the shoulders. Even Bartholomew sinks, sighing as though worn out by the very same drama that had captivated him a moment before.

The weight of Eliza on my chest is suddenly gone.

Everything is dark. My hands rise, rummaging through blanket and sheet, but only the hiss of twisting linen and the scratch of wool greet my blind search.

"Eliza!" I call.

Silence and darkness are my only answers. The name of my lover feels suddenly foolish on my lips. There is no Eliza, no audience either. While part of me is grateful for the latter, there is the smartest of pangs for the loss. If Eliza was not here, then the sensations were a lie. The love and desire that seemed more real than life itself exist not at all beyond the boundaries of my skin. The self-trickery seems cruel beyond understanding. I have been here before, of course. I am not the world's first dreamer and this is not my first dream.

It is not only loss which I fear. One part of the dream, dismissed at the time, is gathering itself afresh in the darkness. Like moles' tunnels which may be viewed by the mounds they make upon the surface of the earth, the pattern of my worries weaves itself through my imagination. *If you let others take your risks,* my dream-Eliza told me, *you must expect others to gather your rewards.*

What others?

There is a creak from Bartholomew's quarters below, and the answer, I decide, is already here. I waste no time.

"Bartholomew!" I bellow into the darkness, sitting up. In swift response there is another creak, a short pause, and then I hear him climbing the stairs, a tread more cautious than usual. Is it guilt that weighs upon him? I try to envision what this, the worst of my fears, would look like turned into the flesh of reality. Eliza, voluptuous as I have just experienced her, not for myself but for the weasel Bartholomew. Do such unspeakable horrors really lurk in the recesses of night? Does decorum and restraint turn to bestial depravity when no witnesses can see?

The crack of light appears, intensifies, and the door swings open. Bartholomew stands in the frame, face and form burning in the candle flame. There is indeed something different about him, I can tell. The bounce and weightlessness of his gait is altered. With shoulders more round, he looks older. This reassures me. He fits not with the image of secret triumph.

"You called me, Mr. Guy?" he says with no effort at pleasing.

"Where have you been?" I ask.

"About your business, sir."

Is it my imagination or is there resentment in his tone?

"Where, precisely?"

"The Egret home. The Crossroads Tavern. The woods on the Avon's north bank. The Crossroads Tavern again."

"This is merely a list, boy!"

"I am merely answering your question, sir."

There is a pause. This is as plainly insolent as he has ever been, and suddenly I realize I don't know what to do about it. I have no hold over him, other than the promise of advancement, and with the dexterity of his brain he might easily achieve that without my help. He is free because I made him so.

"Stay here for a moment, please." I can hear weakness, like some fever, creeping in my voice. Eliza's words from the dream crash over me in a wave: *I cannot be real because you've done nothing to deserve me*. I try to shrug them away as I throw off the rumpled sheets and swiftly begin to dress. "Give me an account of your actions so that I may plan."

"It's done; everything," he says, still at the door. His words, normally mellifluous and floating, drop like heavy weights to the floor. It is very strange.

"What is done?" I ask, fastening my belt. The disingenuousness of the question twists around me like my hastily assembled garments. I know my own instructions. I wonder if the cartwheel-motion in my bowels is the herald of some cowardly impulse to deny them.

"If everything goes to plan, he should be dead before the next nightfall."

The silence is thick as I fasten the buttons of my jacket. I try to fill it with a cough, but it's like a grain of sand in a barrel. Beneath the panic, indignation rises.

"Where's your discretion, man?"

"Discretion, sir?"

"Do not make plain and vulgar that which should be subtle."

I try to stare him down.

The hint of a smile curls his lips.

"The event that you ordered to have brought about, sir," he says more deliberately than I would like, "should be achieved by nightfall if all goes to plan."

"What is your method?" I ask, heat rising around my neck. "Answer in a single word only."

"Belladonna."

"He has taken it already? Yes or no, please."

He pauses. "No."

A number of possibilities, all of them uncomfortable, dance about my brain.

"Answer in a word if you can: how is he to take it without your presence?"

"Helen."

I turn, go to the blinds, and pull them open to skeletal branches, black against the bluish dawn. I turn again to face him. The candle still burns, but he is washed in grey light.

"Answer yes or no: is Helen the innocent, or does she know what she is giving him?"

His tired eyes are filled suddenly with a bitter amusement.

"I cannot answer that question yes or no. It is two-sided."

I feel a rumble in my ears, this time of growing anger.

"Damn you, boy!" I whisper. "Does she know?"

"Yes, Mr. Guy, she knows."

The possibilities dancing in my head take form. Now they are wasps, sharp, buzzing, each harbouring the sting of likely detection.

"You fool!" I fume with the stamp of my foot.

"Pardon me, sir?"

"You were supposed to deal with it yourself."

A smile, sour and penetrating, passes across his face. "Indeed," he says quietly. "Murder should not be subcontracted." He blows out the candle.

My eyes burn now and I turn to the window once more,

viewing scatterings of twigs that reach claw-like into the sky. *I cannot be real because you've done nothing to deserve me.* It is these words, rather than Bartholomew's, which now fizzle and dance in the grey room. My dream-Eliza is right. I have been sneaking toward my prize through a series of back doors and squalid alleyways. A murder is no less bloody for being passed from my hands to those of another. It is the risk itself that gives the act its one gleam of heroism. I have reserved the foulness for myself and given away the sole mitigation of valour.

"We must stop her," I say to the dawn.

"What?" I hear Bartholomew's footfalls padding up behind me. "It may be too late."

His voice is lighter, more like the old Bartholomew. I turn to see his face — eager, nervous, a picture of agitation.

"The route is too circuitous. We will be found out. You must tell her it was merely a joke."

"A joke?" His eyes blink at me like those of a stage clown, but an undercurrent of exasperation is anything but humorous.

"You'll have to think of something."

Before I can add anything more, his shoulders dip and he turns running from the room. I hear his footsteps tumbling down the stairs then running along the hallway. The front door opens and slams.

I turn again to the glass. "Fool!" I whisper at the figure scurrying like a gamecock down the path to the main road. I am full of insults, crueller and more colourful than this one, but I dare not use them for fear they may backfire. Do

I even care about the maid's involvement? Do I think it will expose me to more risk of discovery? The questions melt into nothing next to the words of my imagined Eliza. It's her condemnation of my cowardice allied to the leaden facts — *dead; it's done* — that has turned my head around. There is only one fool here, and it is not Bartholomew.

CHAPTER FIFTEEN

Helen

NESTLING INNOCENTLY IN THE oats and milk, the nightshade is difficult to tell from the overwintered blackcurrants. With each revolution of the spoon the deadly reputation of these frail and thin-skinned berries seems more unlikely, more of a joke.

I watch my hand on the spoon handle, follow the movements of those five bland fingers, the whitish skin, pinker knuckles — no scales, no talons, no sulfur stains. What did Bartholomew say about murder being more common than we think? Glancing up at the wooden shutter that covers most of the pantry window, I steal a peek at the sliver of night beyond, and almost feel the crime slipping into irrelevance. Like a mislaid sewing needle, it may simply skitter along the floor and fall into the cracks of forgetfulness. He has to die sometime, after all. At least the timing — if it is now — might do others some good. What will it matter in ten years or more if he was nudged along the way?

It is nothing, this most feared and vaunted of sins. It is a mere domestic chore, a small handful of drying fruit scattered in my master's breakfast, a task accomplished between yawns.

And then there is Bertha who now whistles through her teeth as she plucks a chicken on the workbench beside me. A short time ago she came up and looked into my palm where nightshade and blackberries mingled together. Although I was about to tip them all into the porridge bowl, Bertha's stare made me stop dead. I even lifted the evidence closer to her eyes, wondering as I did so whether perhaps I wished to be discovered.

"Passed their best, I think," she said with a shake of the head.

"Should we perhaps throw them out?"

I cursed my cowardice as soon as the words left me; an ache of guilt and fear ran from somewhere in my chest, down my poison-laden arm and back again. My fingers trembled and I closed my hand upon the berries before any slipped through.

"No, my dear," she answered, turning and throwing a towel over her shoulder. "The master is pernickety about waste. It's one of his ways to cheat the worm of his reward." She picked up a large pan and moved toward the stove. "But let me take his breakfast to him this morning, in case there are questions. Just because we're following his instructions it doesn't mean he has to be happy about the result."

"Yes," I said hurriedly. I felt lighter then as I threw the berries into his bowl.

I had erected a new obstacle to the crime and Bertha, not I, had dismantled it. Better still, it was she, and not I, who would deliver the fatal blow. Now I could share the crime with *two* others. Only one third of my soul would be damned; hellfire for one third of eternity.

THE PORRIDGE NOW READY, I stop stirring. I turn to Bertha who lifts her hands from the chicken. The sagging bird, abject in its nakedness, seems to wave a half-bald wing at me as Bertha rubs her hands on the towel and takes the bowl.

As she does so, as my fingers slip from the wood, I feel a pang of something new. I watch innocent, kindly Bertha, with her thick ankles, and her many years of stolid, reliable toil, pausing at the table edge to take one of the candles, then shuffling toward the pantry door with a third of my sin. Chain of guilt or no chain, even a third of this crime is more brutally heavy than anything Bertha has ever imagined.

Helpless I watch the door close behind her and the berries, now out of sight, seem no longer innocuous, no longer forgettable, but rather a hundred times more wicked for seeming so. The sudden change within me is like the flutter of a wing, barely felt, but already I feel migrating armies gathering into monster remorse.

In another moment I'm running across the pantry after her, cool sweat creeping under my hairline. As I race up the stairs, syllables of explanation form, scatter, and then form again. Overtaking her halfway up, I reach my hand to the bowl.

"I'll take it to him, Bertha, if you don't mind."

Breathless from the exertion of climbing, she takes a moment to reply. Both of my own hands are now beneath the bowl, but she has made no move to let go.

"I'm almost there, girl, and I have housekeeping questions to talk over with the master."

"Please, Bertha," I say warmly. I make a playful, bouncing action at the knee. This mini-jig of impatience is to remind her of those surrogate years of mother and child. "I need to learn how to deal with the master if he is displeased."

The look she returns to me is warm also, but searching. Her yellow-tinged eyes hold mine for a moment longer than usual. Locked within the same wavering light of Bertha's candle, there is something unthinkable about adding more lies to those I have already constructed, and the sigh as she lets the bowl go does hold a question. But I merely smile, convincingly enough in the circumstances, I think. She holds out the candle for me to take, but I shake my head and gesture for her to keep it. Slowly, she turns to descend, and the warm halo of light follows her. The walls about me flicker, fade, and turn to darkness.

As I start to climb to Mr. Egret's room I find the ache that travelled between my heart and hands in the pantry has dropped now to my feet. My sandals flop after each step, heel and toe landing slightly apart. *Lonely* is the word that the double *flop* spells. Soon a thickening silence gathers around my ears, stretching the time between each footfall, screaming in whispers: *You can't! Turn back! You'll hang!* As in a nightmare where mouths open with urgent but mute warnings, the absence of noise merely heightens the horror. I am the executioner, my shuffling feet seem to say as I reach the landing, yet I am also the condemned.

I raise my fingers to touch Mr. Egret's door and a cool wind blows over me. I imagine the spirit of my mother. Is she urging me onward or turning me back? Once opened there will be no option but to administer the poison. And I will be half a murderess, not merely a third. My mercy for Bertha has lengthened the time of my damnation.

My white hand opens the door before I am aware of a final decision. The palest of light, a hint of dawn only, comes in ghostly streams through the shutters. There is a hiss of silk. The master must have moved upon my entry.

"Is that you, Bertha?"

The question hangs.

I'm not certain why I don't answer. Instead, I make my way in silence toward the shutter on the near wall and open it with one hand, the other still gripping the bowl. Blue light spreads in a wave over the bed. The heavy blanket is smooth over the spare mound of Mr. Egret's body, and the pillow upon which his head now perches is ghostly white.

"Is it morning?" he asks, and I realize why I did not answer. The tone of his voice, thin and wavering, carries an expectation of trouble, and the twin peaks of curiosity and vengeance want to tease this as long as possible. Why should he be anxious? I wonder. Does he fear intruders? Or has he had some premonition? Does he sense assassins in the shadows?

I think of the cool breeze at his door, feel once more the stab of his cane, this time fainter than before. I wonder whether, in the predawn light, I might look like my mother.

"Why don't you answer?" His voice is rising — I can't gauge whether in panic or anger. "Who is it?"

"Isabelle's daughter," I say at last, feeling a heave of regret that I must speak at all, but determined to unearth all guilt. "Helen," I add. "I was trying to give you some light. It is past six o'clock and I have your breakfast."

I approach the bed now and stand a yard or so distant. I do not proffer the bowl yet and Mr. Egret makes no move to take it.

"Why don't you light a candle, girl?" The edge of impatience remains in his voice.

It's only now that I realize how incongruous the darkness feels. I have delivered Mr. Egret's breakfast so many times before dawn, and I have always carried a light. His question is so obvious, my omission so inexplicable, it takes me a moment to gather myself.

"Yes, sir."

I go toward the table by the window, placing the bowl there, then with trembling fingers I unlatch the tinderbox. Sparks rise like small fireworks and finally the candlewick takes. I let the wax drip upon the saucer, and then as I turn the candle upright, the droplet of flame grows into a blade. Fixing the candle base on the saucer, I pick up the bowl and spoon again and shuffle through the glowing light toward the bed.

Grey hairs poke out from beneath his nightcap like hay after an August drought. His pinched and clay-like face makes him seem much older than usual. *These are his last hours*, the portentous words echo in my skull. But there is something forced about it, like a funeral liturgy spoken without the presence of a corpse. It's the silence and calmness that surprise me as I stand before him. He looks at the bowl, his filmy eyes hungry, and his bony fingers reach to receive it. My eyes settle on the white foam in the corner of his lips. Then suddenly, just as his fingertips are about to touch the bowl, I jerk it from his grasp.

His eyes narrow and the reaching hand wavers in mid-air. It's too late already. There is no explanation for the action, none that might see the bowl delivered to him again.

My eyes fix upon the mush of oats and milk-sodden berries.

"Sorry, sir," comes my disembodied gasp, "I saw a maggot in the bowl. I should go and get you a fresh breakfast."

"A maggot, you foolish girl! Are you trying to kill me?"

I'm backing off already. He fades into the blue dawn as the light retreats with me.

"Leave the candle here!"

"Sorry, sir."

I rush toward his night table, put down the light, and then back off once more facing my enemy like a retreating soldier. Groping with one hand I find the door handle, and slip through into the dark space of the landing.

"You're as stupid as your mother!" The words slice through the closing stripe of the door crack.

In the darkness now, holding the untouched, poisoned

food bowl, the reality of failure descends. Moments ago, just after my hand jerked the bowl away, I was thinking not of failure, but of a change of heart. What did this man mean to my mother? the question prodded me. I was acting for her if I was acting for anyone. To kill where she loved was surely a betrayal. Then, when I looked upon my victim with his sunken cheeks, his palsied strands of hair, and the froth of sleep on his lips, angels of pity had swirled in my blood. He was a babe again. No matter his crime, no matter what obstacle to the fortunes of others he might represent, he was defenseless and old. Nothing can blunt the blade of vengeance as swiftly as advanced years. All journeys end in the feebleness of their beginnings, in the spawn of helplessness from which all life rises and to which all life returns. The time for vengeance had passed.

All this I thought in mere moments after withdrawing the poison. Fear makes alibis grow with tenacious speed, with plump leaves and elaborate entwining branches. *Stupid as your mother!* His rusty cane scores me again in the darkness. Did she also try to settle a score? I wonder. Did she make some plea for recognition for herself or for me?

My heart thumps hard. If I could return to him now with the same bowl, I would. But this time he would surely suspect. The discipline of morals weighs upon me like some ungodly chain as I make my way through the descending darkness. The angels of pity were demons in disguise. The spoon bumps against the bowl rim and the thought passes through me that someone must take the poison, so it might as well be me.

CHAPTER SIXTEEN

Bartholomew

"You are rather early, young man."

A smile I would have considered uncharacteristic a day ago passes across Mrs. Egret's face. The housekeeper who admitted me moves quickly out of the main room muttering something about Helen still being upstairs.

I give Mrs. Egret a low bow. "Dear Lady," I tell her, "our time is hardly our own. As your much-honoured late husband must have known, the colonizer does not have leisure for sleep."

"Nor do old women, young sir." As if to illustrate the remark her fingers twitch toward the knitting on her lap. Despite the dawn now showing through the windows, a flame still bobs above her inch-high candle. She must have been up for several hours. "You say it is our Helen you wish to see?"

"Yes, my Lady, if it pleases you."

The same smile comes into her face again, but this time there is a knot of curiosity. I decide to offer some explanation.

"Helen has, we believe, some relatives in the country who have shown an interest in our colony. I wanted to ask her about their skills."

"Relatives in the country," she repeats, weighing the words. "I am aware of no such people, but I suppose you must know your business. She has gone to give the master his breakfast."

Too late, the words echo in my head with sickening reverberations. I attempt a pleasant smile. "So early?"

"So early?" she repeats. "Not too early for you to call, Master Bartholomew."

"Indeed," I say.

"Do take a seat, young sir."

I stare at the vacant chair that stands close by the old lady. My limbs are so agitated, it would seem like imprisonment to sit, but I don't know how to stop Helen and there is little else I can do. I shuffle over and perch myself on the chair's edge. A profound hush descends. Mrs. Egret takes up her knitting again and the pat of the needles is the only sound for some while. I glance sideways at the wavering candle flame.

The flame bobs low as a soft thump comes from somewhere close by. I look up to see Helen, her face ashen, her shoulders slumped and tired. The chair jolts beneath me, the dead wood again spelling the phrase: *too late*.

"You asked to see me, sir."

Although she addresses me, her gaze is locked firmly on the floor, her mouth tight. In the grey light of early morning she seems as far from me as a portrait of a woman long deceased. I wonder how she must view me now I have turned her into a murderess.

"Indeed," I say, rising. "If I may."

"Proceed where you are, young man," says Mrs. Egret without looking up from her knitting. Her words, and the keen observation that accompanied them, give the old lady an unexpected authority and I lower myself once more upon the chair.

I hadn't considered that Mrs. Egret would not let me take the household servant from the room. But then again, why would she? There couldn't be — or *shouldn't* be, at any rate — anything private between us.

"How are you, Helen?" I ask. I am merely playing for time, but the question comes with a splash of sentiment that I distrust.

Her eyes narrow slightly and her gaze remains on the floor.

"Fine, sir," she says.

"And your duties? Am I keeping you from them?"

She winces but this time looks up and catches my eye. It's not the look of anger I was expecting, but something else — desperation, pleading, a sense of urgency that is communicated.

"My duties are done," she says, and I see whiteness in her lips, "all except one which evaded me this morning." She holds my eyes for a moment longer before biting her lip and gazing at the floor.

"Oh?" I ask softly.

"A rat I meant to dispose of. It got away."

A sudden weight falls from my shoulders. My lips itch to know more, but Mrs. Egret, still knitting, beats me to it.

"Helen," she says, "you are like your mother, too soft-hearted."

Helen seems to reel for a moment. There is a glassy look in her eyes when she turns to the old woman.

"I couldn't help it, ma'am," she says. Then, meaningfully, she turns back to me. "It looked at me in the face. I saw its fear."

"The executioner hides his face, Helen," says Mrs. Egret, still looking down at her work. "Otherwise his work would simply go undone."

"Mrs. Egret is right, of course," I say quickly, "you should not be hard on yourself for being tender of disposition."

"But I wanted to have the task accomplished," she says, "now more than ever."

The conviction takes me by surprise and I want to hear more, but again Mrs. Egret breaks in.

"Where are these people of yours, Helen?" she asks. "The ones I hear about?"

Helen's gaze moves from me, to Mrs. Egret, to a beam high above the family crest, then back to me. I edge forward, not knowing quite how to interrupt.

"Ma'am?" she asks after what seems an age.

"Your relatives in the country," says Mrs. Egret. It may be

my imagination, but her needles seem to clack together with more force than before.

"Helen," I blurt. "I mentioned my mission to Mrs. Egret. That you have people in the country who might be interested in working in Cupers Cove."

"Oh," she says softly.

"Perhaps you can get them to rid you of the rat, Helen," says Mrs. Egret. And now I am sure. The movements of her fingers are more swift and decisive even if her voice is measured. The needles clink like falling icicles. "You know I came from the country to the east of Bristol and we had a custom in winter. Everyone would dress from head to toe in a disguise and roam from house to house."

"The mummers," I say.

"Exactly, young man: the mummers." Her small, grey eyes dart up at me for a second. "And mostly it was fine sport."

"Mostly, ma'am?"

She stops her knitting and begins to unpick a thread. "Mostly, young sir. But when there was something to settle, it was a different matter. The troupe of mummers would draw lots, and the loser would deliver punishment, swift and sure. When the disguises were off, no one was any the wiser about whom had delivered the blow."

She lays her knitting upon her lap, smiles, and closes her eyes as though remembering the most golden of times. For the second time in less than the sun's full cycle it seems the old lady has opened the door to murder.

CHAPTER SEVENTEEN
Matilda

WHAT IS THIS STRANGE poison of mine that seeps into the world regardless of any decision on my own part? Yesterday morning's interview with Mr. Guy and his young companion provided the motivation for murder and, implicitly at least, even my blessing. Now I have gone much further. I have counselled the young people on their mistakes and suggested a new approach.

Now, alone once more, the pale morning streaming through the windows, I trace the thread of the conversation between Bartholomew, Helen, and I, trying to fix upon an innocent interpretation. It is no use. We all knew we were talking about more than rats and mummers. The young man's soft footfalls, the hush in his voice as he bowed and made his way to the door; the way Helen followed him, so unlike any maid, skirts shuffling close by his side, shoulders hunched in whispering confidences, left no doubt. I knew. They knew. We each saw knowledge in the other.

Had the true purpose for his visit been less obvious, I might not have spoken as I did. Like a schoolmaster obliged to unearth a pupil's covert behaviour, I spoke the language of their true desires better than they could have spoken it themselves. But while a good teacher would have used knowledge to shame the miscreant, to spread the light of wisdom and virtue on the darkness of subterfuge, I did the opposite. I began to excavate deeper, to elaborate on the labyrinthine tunnels of their code.

I know why they called my brother-in-law a rat. He scurries and runs from peril and guards a horde that is only partly his. He bites with a mean, quick temper, keeping from the house any perceived danger, even if that danger might bring joy to his dead brother's widow. I think of Philip and Nicholas, of the joyful years and the trickles of laugher that might still have come my way even as a widow. A rat indeed.

Then what am I? I who tease and deepen the vices of the young, insinuating myself into their world then pulling upon a thread to make the would-be murderer think again before abandoning his goal?

I must be a spider, a creature of merciless patience that weaves and plans but does not like to expose the extent of her control. Such power as I have lies in the fact that I am unnoticed.

Like a spider, I must now wait. "The mummers will come tonight, ma'am," was the young man's warning, or perhaps his promise.

I looked at Helen as he spoke. She stood close to young Bartholomew, staring into his eyes, as if she was ready to declare her love before the world. Terror and anticipation were in her face. Her fingers rose to lift a hair wisp from her forehead. Frightened as she was, there was consent in her silence. Maid, gentleman; the façade of such roles fell away.

Was I not looking into the mirror of the past and seeing myself and Nicholas as we were thirty years ago? We were different in many particulars from the young people standing before me now. The dangers of travel and the trials of waiting were enough for us without the weight of mortal sin. But this change in intensity is merely part of the natural course. For each generation the forfeit must increase, or how can the son outdo his father?

"If you wish to borrow our maid for your plans, young man, go ahead," I broke into their hushed leave-taking. "I'm sure Bertha will manage the household well enough."

"Thank you, ma'am," Helen replied, stepping before her companion and toward the door.

"No," replied her young man in an urgent whisper. "You can't be part of this!" He cast a sidelong glance in my direction, unaware it seemed that I caught every word. It is my curse perhaps that my hearing is as acute as ever. I know from the creak of a door a storey below when servants come and go. The wonder of it all has kept me awake these last two nights.

"I am part of it already," she told him more quietly still, but I caught the words again. "I have to share this with you. I can't explain why."

CUPIDS

She tugged at his sleeve and, reluctantly, he seemed to relent. In any case they did leave together, and since the house fell into silence again I have felt a stirring in my belly. The spirit of Nicholas has returned to me at last. Together we have set our proxies on their quest.

CHAPTER EIGHTEEN

Guy

CANDLELIGHT SKIMS ACROSS THE opening above me. At last I can see, as well as sense from the boxed-in feeling at my shoulders, the shape of the receptacle within which I lie. The dry oak measures out a hollow oblong, deep and foreboding.

The flame is encouraging at least. I cannot begin to guess how long I have been incarcerated, nor do I know which drug has prevented movement for this passage of time. But the golden light, the glimpse of wormholes close to the rim, even the confirmation of what I already knew, that this place of confinement is a coffin, is welcome after a whole phase of existence in darkness.

A white-gloved hand gathers itself at the rim — finger joining finger until it perches like a giant spider, palm down, and ready to make a spiralling descent. The light becomes sharper and I hear a soft breath.

Eliza's face comes into view, her eyes turquoise in the flame, her hair more golden than the setting of her father's pendant. The candle itself appears. Dripping wax oozes over the white-gloved hand that holds the shaft.

"My poor Guy," she says softly.

There is such a real sadness, and even a slight moistening of her eyes, that I struggle for a reply, something that might strive to be worthy of her sympathy. Phrases tumble into my imagination — *no longer poor . . . my dear Eliza . . . with you to gaze upon* — but my mouth can't move to voice them; my jaws open but my lips remain closed. My tongue turns helplessly like a worm struggling upon a hook.

"Don't try to speak, it's over," she says in the same caressing tones. "Poor man, you can't act to get your wish. You can't even delegate without a sudden change of mind. Still, you deserve something for thinking of me."

The hand on the coffin lifts to join the one holding the candle. As both sets of fingers move up and down the candle, streams of wax ooze faster, spilling over her gloves until she smiles, lays the candle upon some unseen surface beyond my coffin, and shakes her gloves free of those drops yet to congeal.

She turns from the coffin. As her face gradually comes into view again, I hear a scraping as of wood against wood. Only when she backs off a little and slides the long, flat object to partially block the space above me, do I realize the thing she has been dragging is the coffin's lid. She picks up the candle again and holds it in the narrowing space between us.

"Now my not-so-brave knight," she says, her face a sweet smile beside the fluttering flame, "I'll say goodnight."

The lid slams into a complete horizontal then judders along inch by inch until the light above me narrows to a slit. Like those of a drowning man, my lungs fill, and when the slit disappears, thunder reverberates through my body. If all the air in the world were available to me now, I think I would draw it all into myself. I would hold it in storage for myself. Others might use it, but only if I am pleased at the nature of their request. Life now ebbing from me, I have no dearer wish than to be the gatekeeper of life itself.

My fingers ache to move, but they are helpless. My lips tingle with the impulse of one last hope, that if I can call her name, if I can draw her into some conversation, I might save myself. The tip of my tongue quivers against the insides of my lips, searching for a way through.

And then I hear it, that dread sound — *thump, thump, thump* — of nail into wood: the sound of irreversible death.

At last I feel it coming. From the back of my neck, a rising squeal, not a human sound at all but a breaking seam in the thousand-ton silence which oppresses me. The pressure in my lungs breaks; my jaws fly open, parting my lips. Every sinew, muscle, and nerve — every hair and every nail of my fingers and toes — launches into the same black tunnel of sound.

Counter-swirls dance upon the main thrust of the roar, circling and reforming, frothing into an unnamable, husky, throat-ripping shriek. I did not plan for a word, but the word that emerges is one I recognize once it has resounded and echoed beyond my own body: *Eliza!*

Then I am awake. The sound, it seems, was enough to propel me from one world to another, to shatter the coffin and dissolve its constituent parts, to blow away the ghostly Eliza and her candle, to turn night into day.

I push myself up from the breakfast table, the orange lights of morning swirling before me. A string of drool hangs from my chin, and my ears sing from the extraordinary noise I have just emitted.

Bartholomew and the maid stand before me, startled.

I quickly dab my chin with my sleeve.

"Well?" I ask, my voice strained and husky.

"Well?" Bartholomew echoes.

"What news?"

Bartholomew and Helen look at each other. I see no smirks, but a thousand meanings dance somewhere beneath their expressions. The easy nuance between them irks me. Everything beneath the surface is subversive, and collectively they know far too much about me.

"I caught her in time," Bartholomew says. "I didn't tell her it was a joke. I thought you might want to explain that part yourself."

I think of standing. I feel a fresh roar of anger gathering and my legs twitch in preparation. But a moisture nestling among the hairs of my thigh persuades me it might be unwise, and that the terror of my nightmare might well have unmanned me in ways I would not have exposed.

"A joke?" asks Helen.

"I'm afraid we might have lacked the courage of our convictions," Bartholomew tells her. "And that we have worked too hard to cover our tracks."

"I don't know what you mean by that, young man," I tell him hoarsely. Frustrated in anger, I feel my energies settling rather upon pride. No more delegating. No more hiding. "It was not my plan to involve the Egrets' own household, that's all. Young woman, this is not your concern."

Something fires in the maid's eyes, not quite anger, but a quality harder and less warm. "Pardon me, sir," she says, moving a step sideways from Bartholomew, "but it is my concern, and between you, you have made it so."

"I don't understand," I tell her. "What is it that you want?"

She pauses, in hesitation it seems, but then her shoulders move forward like those of a hawk spotting its prey. "To have done the thing I meant to do this morning. To have it done, sir, not to say, or plan, or change our minds and plan again, to go through tortures of rethinking, and doubt, and after it all leave the thing itself undone. To do it and have it done!"

Silence hangs in the room. I see dust specks tumble in the late winter light, and suddenly it makes sense. I can see how Bartholomew and I, like incompetent hunters, might well slip once, twice, and slip yet again and let our quarry free. Failure, once established, would be the easier course, one that requires so little in the way of change. With this young woman — whatever her motives might be — we may be forced to succeed.

Bartholomew shifts his rather mournful gaze from Helen to me.

"We believe we have the method."

CHAPTER NINETEEN

Helen

WILL YOU BE THE one? These are the words the hemp fibres murmur as I pull the rope tighter around my waist.

It's odd that we are back to three again, the mystic number, it seems, when it comes to murder. I wonder whether some clause exists in the great book of damnation through which the third-part assassin may plead for mercy. If it is me, at least I can share my crime with Bartholomew. If it is him, at least he can share his guilt with me. The fact there is another still, that Mr. Guy may have to perform his own assassination, is a hope upon which I daren't dwell.

Mr. Guy's house is so silent. I hear the softest of creakings beneath my own sandals in this loft, but the moan of the wind beyond the tiny window causes no yelp of beam, no skittering of stones or pebbles from the roof, and I hear no voices from below. Each of my companions in crime must be dressing alone without words. I find myself longing for Bartholomew, longing for time not spent upon the tightrope of danger, but of languid, slow hours spent at nature's pace, walking upon emerald hills in spring, fingers skimming across the furry heads of dandelions. Does our future hold any such promise? I try to imagine the tremulous void of the present giving way to days of sunshine and laughter and it hardly seems possible.

I think of Newfoundland, the shimmer of mermaids under the summer moon, the kiss of spiced air. I am aware that Bartholomew's silver tongue deceived when he spoke of the place. Still the very name promises a new beginning, and this is where life will likely take us after the deed is accomplished. Surely murder cannot follow so far.

I know it is we who carry our crimes, but I know also the human form can expand and change. Imagination can engender plays and music, the green leaves of poetry, societies both make-believe and real. Man and woman can quite literally spill new lives upon the earth. Why should a minus one cancel out a plus five or six? And five or six, in generations to come, will expand in the general pool to five or six hundred. "More common than you think," Bartholomew said when he spoke of murder. And it may be true. Murder is common enough in the Bible. Did not Abraham mean to sacrifice Isaac? Did not Cain dispose of Abel, his brother? Yet the descendants are not damned, but blessed. From the distance of history, crime is nothing more than the price we pay to fate.

A shuffle sounds upon the stairs and I listen sharply to the flop of sandals outside the door. Three knocks sound upon the wood.

"I'm ready," I call out, breathless. "Come in."

The robed form that enters is myself. I realize Bartholomew has chosen our costumes well. He pulls back his monk's hood and stands before me, shoulders slumped and eyes bleary and red. Still, there is a hint of humour in his expression as he regards me.

"We're ready to draw lots," he says.

I nod and move toward him, surprised at the nerves which dance along my limbs as though in tune to the itch of the sackcloth.

"I want you out of the draw," he says as I reach him. "It should be either me or Guy." I'm surprised by the paleness of his face, the darkness under his eyes. The very breath that reaches me, though soft and moist, seems tinged with sudden care.

"For the last time, Bartholomew," I tell him, "I am in."

His left eye twitches and the heavy lids blink.

"Why?" The question comes in a breath.

"I want to share the reward of your success," I tell him, feeling the sting of mendacity on my cheek. I wonder if I will ever tell him about Mr. Egret and my mother, about my likely parentage. "I'm returning with you to Newfoundland." Now the heat in my face intensifies, but for the opposite reason; I am naming my true desire. "To do so in conscience, I must share the inherent dangers of the task to the full."

He nods weakly and raises his hand to my elbow. The

fingers drop before they make contact with the sackcloth, but it feels like enough. He turns slowly to the door and I with him. We pass into the landing and together descend the narrow staircase.

CHAPTER TWENTY

Bartholomew

THE TRUST OF THE girl touches me so deeply it hurts. What have I given her but the shadow of criminality? What have I promised? Even my lustful advances dissolved into an assassin's blade. How low must be her expectations, how desperate her need to escape!

With the double pat of sandal against stone — a timorous heartbeat under the high ceiling of Guy's main parlour — I feel a change within me, a feeling that the true meaning of the ceremony we are about to undertake has inverted. This is a pact deeper than any marriage vow. Guy, who stands motionless and hooded before the table, is our witness and priest. The spoken intent between Helen and I — to share our dangers and riches, fortune and misfortune — echoes perfectly the very essence of union between woman and man. Only the element of sacrifice stands out as a pagan smear. But, then again, these are trying times, and in such times the nerve must tighten to prepare for an assault on the tender senses. Has not growth, renewal, and hope always been connected with the spilling of blood? Does not the egg perish after the hatching of the chick? I try to envision the new life that this strange union between Helen and I will produce. The most usual image — bawling infant with tight-closed eyes and clamped, pink fists — comes into my seeing and leaves just as quickly. I remember the Crossroads Tavern, how my hands pulled at the folds of her nightdress, gathering the fabric into my palms, and how the seduction was cut short. Or were my hands exploring because they knew I would not have to deliver their suggested intent, that weightier matters would intervene? The whispers of Cupers Cove return, and I listen to all the taunts — *think you're something, better than us* — along with the suggestion that my presence alone was a temptation beyond enduring and that I inflamed evil desire without ever quenching its thirst. Will I ever be able to deliver the promises I have made to Helen?

As I take my place at the table's head, Guy doesn't oppose me. My head still buzzes with his most recent attempt to shirk the crime of his ambitions, and I check his posture to see if he's wavering again.

"I've been thinking," he told me less than half of an hour ago as I proffered him one of the monk's robes I found by raiding the theatre's storage room. He did not take the garment and straightaway I knew there was trouble.

"Sir?" As I spoke the word, weariness, as well as impatience, burned upon my lips. We were in Guy's study. Helen had already gone upstairs without a word of complaint. My arm ached under the weight of the sackcloth.

"The course you have mapped out is too treacherous, too uncertain. Egret's death does not guarantee permanent success for the colony."

I kept my arm extended, but his eyes would not drop from my face to his disguise. His hands remained on his desk as though the level oak steadied his thoughts.

"But, sir," I told him, "it does guarantee you control of real wealth for one and a half years, and such influence over her fortune that Eliza will surely see you as the very wellspring of pleasure. True affection will surely follow comfort."

He straightened his back and sighed, still gripping the corners of the desk. The action, suggesting as it did the weight of the world, made my lips tremble with inchoate rage. *You coward!* I wanted to yell at him. Instead I tipped my head to one side politely as though to elicit a response.

"I don't know that for sure," he murmured.

"Sir," I said with a calmness belied only by the splash of a tear on my lower lash, the moisture of pure fatigue. "The young do not look beyond the season they are in." I took a step toward him so that the monk's costume rumpled against his arm. "And in any case, everything is arranged. We have the costumes. We have the means to inflict his death. I have even hired actors and musicians to join us also in disguise. Our real purpose, known only to we three, will be buried under wave upon wave of deception."

He sighed again, eyes in movement. I knew him well enough by now, I'd been here often enough. He was almost persuaded but required one last argument.

"Sir," I whispered. "Success is a ladder. The rungs are climbed not in foreknowledge of all consequences, but one at a time and in ever-increasing hope. If your mind stays upon the present, the future will look after itself."

He looked down at the costume, at the thick rope dangling upon his rug. And slowly, reluctantly, with a sigh, he moved to take it at last. And Guy's plan, Guy's ambition, Guy's infatuation with the Egret daughter, became once more *my* idea.

HOW SWEET HELEN SEEMS to me now — a woman who takes my own darkness upon herself and carries it with such conviction — as she stands eyes intent on the slates before me.

"I will chalk the letter 'M' upon one of these three slates," I say, looking first at Helen and then at Guy. Launching into the explanation, I feel a tingle in my shoulders, a late realization perhaps that I could have backed out when Guy expressed his latest doubt, and with puzzlement at myself that I did not even consider this. Like so many times before, I allowed another's expectations of me to take over. I am the tempter, and Guy must feel as though he has been talked into it.

"All three slates," I continue, "will be turned over so the letter will not be seen. I will change their positions when your backs are turned. Then each of you will pick a slate, and I will take the last. He or she who picks the letter 'M' is the one who must perform the deed."

Guy pulls back his hood, revealing a face knotted with suspicion.

"It is the safest, fairest method I know, Mr. Guy."

Suspicion fades to a lip-twitching fear, and he gives a slight nod. What a fool the man is!

CHAPTER TWENTY-ONE

Matilda

A<small>LL</small> <small>DAY AND</small> <small>ALL</small> evening I've been listening for them, hardly knowing what sound might herald their coming. For the last hour rainless thunder has growled over Bristol like a warning from some colossal dog. Only during the last few minutes has nature's fury been joined by another, even less welcome, noise — the crackle of hot fluid as my brother-in-law sucks the gruel from his spoon. The steady, rhythmic tremble of the bauble which hangs from Mr. Egret's silk nightcap ticks away relentlessly at the last minutes of his waking. I look hard upon my knitting, at the busy hands that have spun the plot, and wonder if my conspirators have left it too late.

Bertha has orders to admit them. Even my brother-in-law himself gave grudging consent to the idea of mummers. His reaction to the news of their visit was a characteristic wince, a thin-lipped snarl and then a softening of the eyes, as though the notion of mummers came from an area of his past, so remote and so distant he didn't dare deny it. It was like witnessing the heart of a miser thawed by remembrance of his mother's long-forgotten cradle song.

There is an almighty crash and long-sustained grumble that sends emissaries of noise like heaven-spilled anger, small booms and rivulets of tinny clashes. These sounds, which parody the scale of the boom from which they grew, seem not of the sky at all, but are rather oddly skimming along the earth from the direction of Broad Quay. They are joined first by the most tuneless of trumpet blasts, then by cacophonic blowing of flutes, and finally by the steady tramp of feet. One, two, three further blasts of all the instruments together, each time closer to the house, tumble into a loud drum roll, then a single very loud rap upon the front door.

This is it, I realize. My hands cease their work, purplish fingers twitching once, and then resting. The bauble on my brother-in-law's nightcap dangles as his head rises from his gruel, then stills.

The rap comes a second time and a loud voice booms through the oak.

"Any mummers, I say, any mummers 'lowed in?"

Bertha, red-faced with excitement, emerges from the pantry shuffling through the main room to the door. She lifts the heavy latch, opens the door wide, and steps to one side.

A scarlet-faced devil garbed in flowing black silk strides into the room, pitchfork held like a walking stick in one hand. Two "imps," either children or little people, slip their flutes into their tunic pockets and begin turning cartwheels around their master. The devil bows at Bertha, I, and Mr. Egret, and then turns his red mask toward the still-open door. In comes a hooded monk, a chalice in hand, followed by a fantastic bird-drummer with a long raven beak, slit eyes, and shimmering multicoloured ribbons as feathers. The bird-drummer takes its place beside the devil and beats an accompaniment to the procession. Another hooded monk enters, a wavering-flamed candle held in one black-gloved hand. Then comes a man-sized donkey with quivering ears and a trumpet held in its forehoof. A third hooded monk with dipping flame slips in close behind the donkey, then a fluting harlequin with a bird-like mask with two more imps tumbling on his heels, one with flute, one with trumpet and drum.

Bertha closes the front door and stares in wonder. As the cool air settles, a constant movement of colour now begins. The imps — no longer tumbling — pipe and dance and drum together. The donkey, the shimmering bird, and one of the monks do the same. The devil and two monks make another whirling triangle. My eyes blur with the candle flames, the devil's red mask and black, silken robe, and the shimmering multicoloured ribbons. The steps are not from any particular dance, but seem to hold a parody of them all: a courtly nod and turn upon a change of tempo in the cacophonic music suggests intricate and formal observance. The bird shimmers a low bow to the group opposite as though in deep appreciation of their skill. Music speeds and partners change, a monk and the devil switching groups. All the while the harlequin looks on, holding the flute by the fingertips and gesturing at the three dancing groups as though it is all too exquisite for words.

Mr. Egret looks on, his thin fingers tapping the table by his gruel bowl. His lips twist into a smile. I tear my gaze from him, eyes stinging from the jagged lines the candle flames etch through the air. The faintest of impulses — a twitch of the fingertips, a tickle in the root of my hair — prods me to intervene. But I know I will not. It is merely that I do not want to witness what will surely now pass. I no longer feel the architect of the deed about to be performed. An accumulation of fate dictates the crime, not I. I am merely the gatekeeper who clicked open a lock that was bound to rust and drop free with time. It's the horror of blood that I fear; the scream of pain and the startled accusation; and shows of grief too. I'm so glad Eliza is away tonight.

Suddenly the music ceases, except for the drum, upon which the bird now thumps at long, ominous intervals. The mummers all gather in a semicircle around my brother-in-law.

The devil raises his pitchfork.

"Worthy, Mr. Egret," he calls in the clear and perfect diction of a stage performer addressing a packed auditorium. "You have sent the light of exploration into darkness unknown. The flame of knowledge is yours!"

A monk steps forward and timorously hands Mr. Egret the candle with bobbing flame. My brother-in-law takes it willingly enough and lays it to the side of his bowl. The monk retreats into the circle again.

"Gracious, Mr. Egret," the devil announces, raising his pitchfork once more, "you have sought wealth for your fellows and yourself through good enterprise in foreign parts. The flame of prosperity is yours!"

A second monk shuffles forward; the wobbling candle drips onto the cloth of a trembling black glove. Mr. Egret takes this candle also and lays it beside the other. Each flame gains strength from its fellow once the candle base is upon a flat surface. The two burn high and strong together.

"Honest, Mr. Egret," the devil says with a flourish. "You have launched adventures from our fine city, and have stood by the valiant both in failure and success. The wine of their mixed fortunes is yours!"

A third monk approaches softly with the chalice, nods at Mr. Egret and offers it. My brother-in-law nods in return and comes as close to a genuine smile as I have ever seen. Is it possible, I wonder, that from his low vantage point he can make out the features of the monk through the dark opening allowed by the hood? He even raises the chalice in a salute first to this monk, and then to all the mummers as the monk shuffles back into line. Then he tips back his head and drinks, Adam's apple bobbing up and down before he lowers the goblet and leans back in his chair in happy reverie.

The whole troupe yells and claps in unison, except, it seems, for the three monks who stand unmoving, dark hoods crumpling lower than before. Then quickly, and as though on military order, all the mummers join hands and skip — banging, fluting, and trumpeting — in a circle around the table and then in a curving train toward the door.

Bertha, eyes shining and delighted at the effect they have had upon her master, opens the door to their progress. She claps at the final few blasts as bird, then harlequin, then two monks together, then imp, then monk again, then devil, and then imps again disappear, tumbling into the night. Bertha takes her time about closing the door, and I hear the music cease and a rumble of voices rise.

"I should get more than an eighth of the fee," complains the devil in his unmistakable clipped tones. "I had all the lines."

"What about this costume?" is the reply, I presume from either the bird or the donkey.

"Being uncomfortable isn't the same as acting . . ."

The argument fades into the darkness. Bertha turns with a happy sigh and leans back, closing the door at last.

She looks to Mr. Egret, as do I.

"Mummers!" he says, staring into some unseen distance, the moisture of fresh sentiment in his eyes. The goblet, still clasped in his hand, sinks farther into his chest and tips sideways. Bertha moves toward him instinctively, ready to save any spill. Then she stops a little way from him.

"Mr. Egret, sir."

The glaze has appeared to settle on my brother-in-law's eyes. His face, still a smile, has stiffened oddly in the corners of his mouth, and the goblet tips a little farther in the grip of unfeeling hands.

"Mr. Egret," she repeats, this time a frantic note creeping into her voice. Strange, and rather selfish of me really, not to consider how Bertha might grieve him. I'd like to save her the next few minutes and pass on the plain fact that she will discover eventually through mirrors, feathers, and close listening to his chest, all the while experiencing the torments of uncertainty and hope. But I can't do that, I realize, without giving myself away.

"What appears to be the matter, Bertha dear?" I ask her.

She turns to me like a lost child, her eyes large and terrified. Her lips begin to move, but nothing but the softest of murmurs reaches my ears.

"Bertha, dear," I say in a comforting a tone, "perhaps you should fetch a doctor."

CHAPTER TWENTY-TWO

Guy

THREE DAYS, THREE DAYS, three days — the sound accompanies each crunch and lift of my footsteps upon the Egret path. The last thin mist of morning rises around me like the living breath of a new creation. Is it too soon? I wonder, gazing up at the shuttered windows as they loom above me, drawing closer. Or is it perhaps too late?

Rarely in my life have I felt so near to losing control as I did when watching Richard, that young dandy cousin of Eliza's, minister to her at the funeral — a kerchief here, a courtly offer of his hand there, and the coldest of stares for me. He no doubt resented the unexpected power I have gained over the Egret money. But the last laugh will surely be mine.

The silt and pebbles gathering under my soles add skittering words to my chant: *Three days since the funeral; three more since his death.* Now I have come to collect.

Eliza will understand. She well knows that the lives of colonists cannot wait; the ways of commerce and travel, swift and obeying their own urgent tides, surely flow in her veins. I lift the cold iron knocker and let it drop, and try as I do so to chase away my remaining fear with arguments of necessity. I must act now. Our ship is ready, supplies purchased. The womenfolk are mustered and waiting. At present they are merely mouths, feeding upon the enterprise to which they will later contribute labour and comfort. The last and most unsavoury remnants of the business have been settled away, clearing my course. After a brief and silent panic over questions of cause, the death certificate was signed and duty paid, and the lifeless husk of the deceased interred. The rogue Bartholomew has received the stock I promised. He can either sell it for gold or barter it for supplies should he wish to begin his own venture in the new world as he implied he might.

The thought of Bartholomew coils inside me like a knot as I wait for the sound of footsteps within. Was it my imagination or did he suggest he might return to Cupers Cove? The idea is unendurable and possesses the carrion reek of blackmail. The danger he represents haunts me like a shadow. The man and his betrothed are still in my house and I wonder if I will ever shake him free. I feel the stubborn prick of the thorniest of regrets. I could in the earliest planning stages have made it a condition of the deal that he must remain in England.

The door creaks open slowly and Bertha appears still white-faced and red-eyed. A chilly feeling wafts over me and drains me for the moment of my composure.

"I have business to discuss with Miss Eliza," I say, unnecessarily, it seems. Bertha, good soul, has already stepped aside to let me in.

As I enter the main room the image of Mrs. Egret, hunched more than usual over her knitting, skims against my eye. I cannot look at her directly. My gaze settles upon Eliza. Dressed in black with black lace, her face ghostly pale even in the strong golden light of the fire by which she sits. In her white quivering fingers she holds a book of psalms.

I wait for a moment to see if she will look up at me but, except for the verses before her, she seems quite unconscious of her surroundings. I cough and give a short bow.

"My Lady, I come to pay my respects."

"Oh! Mr. Guy." The book flutters in her hand and drops to her lap. Her exclamation, sudden as it is, holds a tingle of pleasure for me. "I wasn't expecting anyone."

Her lips curl into a sweet, sad smile and in the blueness of her eyes I cannot help but sense a longing.

"My dear Eliza," the words spill without my foreknowledge. The tremble in my thighs makes me wonder if they mean to collapse me into kneeling. For the moment at least they hold me upright.

Eliza's face remains kindly and inviting. The hint of puzzlement softens rather than mars the genial perfection of her beauty.

"Thank you for that, Mr. Guy," she says in a manner far more formal than I might have wished, her lips downturning with the sourness of distaste. She is in deep mourning, after all, I tell myself, and must retain full decorum. She continues in measured tones. "I have received many of the most courteous and attentive gestures from those who share our great loss. I'm sure I will count your kindnesses among them."

That damn shield again! My legs no longer ache to drop me to the floor. Instead I am held rigid against my will as though a steel pole were lodged along my spine.

"My dear Miss Eliza," I begin once more, stiff yet determined to break through. "I come to tell you my ship is almost ready, and our new voyage to Cupers Cove will soon begin."

"Ah." She smiles brightly and I am momentarily lost in confusion. "And is your excellent young friend Master Bartholomew to sail with you or will he remain and entertain us?"

My lips tighten. "I'm afraid," I murmur quickly, "at this moment I cannot say."

"I hear he might take our maid on his adventures." Her eyes narrow, and wistfully she adds, "There's part of me that envies her now."

"Who knows about Bartholomew?" I say rather too boldly. Then, in tones more calm but no less emphatic, I continue, "It is of matters regarding myself that I have come to speak."

I hear Mrs. Egret's needles clanking together in the silence. The remnants of Eliza's smile disappear altogether but she blinks and she seems to ready herself for listening. "I am sorry, Mr. Guy. I had forgotten for the moment that my aunt thought it best to give you the reins of her estate until

I am twenty. You must have a hundred matters of business to discuss."

"Only one," I tell her. The blood rushing in my ears feels like a river about to burst its banks. "And I wonder if I may crave your aunt's indulgence for a moment and ask for a brief private interview with you."

For the first time I turn to Mrs. Egret. The kiss of hot shame upon my face tells me it is more out of fear of looking directly at Eliza than in courtesy to the old woman that I have switched my gaze. Mrs. Egret does not look up, nor does her posture alter save for a slight bending of the shoulders and rising of the needles and wool as though in extra attention to the task.

"You may not crave my aunt's indulgence," says Eliza with entrail-withering decisiveness. Do I see a slight frown come into and then pass from Mrs. Egret's expression?

I turn to Eliza. A faint yellow star appears and disappears in the line of my eyes. My vision of Eliza tilts and then corrects. "My aunt, dear sir, is now my closest legal confidant and counsel. I cannot discuss matters of great importance without her wise advice."

I steady myself quickly, rooting my feet upon the floor. *Great importance,* she said. Her gaze in my direction is earnest, direct and intelligent. Is this not the very manner in which a sensible woman would wish to receive a proposal of marriage — especially one she means to seriously entertain? Would she also not need the company of the one who would be first from whom the couple must seek consent — particularly if the answer is yes?

The urge to kneel returns and this time I find my legs obeying. Eliza's eyes widen as I descend and draw closer. *Widen*, I note; the very word signifies an opening and an acceptance.

"Dearest Eliza," I begin, thankful of the clearness and the confidence in my voice. Mrs. Egret's needles beat a steady and somewhat comforting rhythm, and I wonder if it's possible that the old lady has spoken to her niece in my favour already. "For 'dearest Eliza' is how I intend to address you for evermore if you should look favourably upon my most humble and sincere of suits." I meet the unmoving clearness of her gaze with my own. The blue in her eyes contracts and expands in wave-like motions at the expense of the black within, and there is something fine and delicious in her inscrutability, something delightful in the maturity that does not giggle or run in triumph to a gaggle of friends but listens as one adult to another. "I ask you, dear Eliza, to do me the very great honour of becoming my wife."

The words are swallowed by silence, save for the clink of Mrs. Egret's knitting. Eliza's bottom lip twitches slightly. I wonder if my speech was perhaps rather too short, but gathering the strands and finding a way back in after such an obvious climax seems beyond me, at least for the moment. Then something takes me by surprise, something so swift, so unaccountable that at first I imagine a dove has scooped in through the window and flown wing-first into my left ear and cheek. It is only when I notice that the blow was undeniably connected to a movement of Eliza's right arm, when my ear sings in a manner that recalls punishment in the schoolroom, and when I look to see that no dove lies stricken at my knees, that I realize the true explanation. No sooner has my brain begun to absorb this than the same thing occurs a second time, this time slowly enough to appreciate and follow the event as it unfolds. Her arm is raised. Her hand sweeps through the air and smacks hard against the left side of my head. My ear sings another, slightly higher note, and the two remain in harmony as one rises and another fades.

One hope stirs, feeble at first like a dying leaf in winter, but gaining strength already from the rich nutrients of my imagination. I have heard it said that in women anger and love are close in kinship, and that violence cannot exist in the bosom of woman without the presence of other passions. For the moment, though, silence reigns. One of my knees scrapes against the floor in preparation for rising. Words once more begin to tumble before I can stop and weigh them.

"I feel I must crave your forgiveness, my Lady. I had no intention of offending." My body rises like some dead thing animated by an unnatural far-off force, shoulders sloping, hands like numb claws.

"How could you do anything but offend?" Her voice, though quiet enough, carries the strength of venom. "You, who try to make love when the whole city is in mourning, you, with hands soiled with the grime of work, you who presume so far above your station merely because you have the good fortune to administer the funds of your superiors. How could you be so deceived to think the daughter of the gentleman who has supped with the traders of Venice and Tuscany could even look upon one who commands only a few dozen men and toils with pigs and goats?"

The final word is spat out with more contempt than I would have thought possible for such an innocent and nondescript animal. The burgeoning hope about anger and passion which had begun to twitch into new life is suddenly limp and dead. As I turn to leave, one ear still singing, Mrs. Egret's needles still clicking quietly in the other, I realize that I myself now drag a mountain of thwarted passion and there is nowhere in the world where I may place it.

CHAPTER TWENTY-THREE

Bartholomew

SPRING IS PALPABLE NOW. Ghostly fingers of mist rise on the road beyond Guy's home. I'm not sure why I should feel so responsible, but deep inside me is some fretting parent awaiting the return of a foolish child.

Helen draws to the window beside me.

"We should get ready to leave," I tell her. My breath fogs the pane.

"We're almost packed," she replies, and I can sense a question hovering in the air between us like a cloud of mosquitoes. It is *the* question, perhaps, the one I have somehow managed to evade for six days. "I wanted to thank you," she says, and momentarily I'm wrong-footed.

"Thank me?" I whisper. She draws closer to my shoulder and I feel my body half turn in response. "What for?"

"I've been afraid to talk about it before, afraid of giving any voice to the deed."

"You are right to leave the deed in silence."

"Then I will talk only of its prelude: the slates — your method of drawing lots."

I was right. It is *the* question. I am fastened to the spot and the dust of my evasion swirls in vain searching for an escape.

"I remember your trick with the pendant, and with the sovereign."

"Yes?"

"You could easily have dictated who received the slate marked 'M.'"

I pause, reluctant to give voice to the admission.

"I want to thank you for not choosing me."

A small, involuntary laugh of reprieve bounces from me. This is not quite the question I was dreading, but it's close enough. "You are more than welcome, Helen," I say, hoping to distract her with the ardour in my voice. "I would hardly foist such a task upon my own future wife."

"I knew it was deliberate, of course," she says, "and this is what makes it so puzzling." I see her breath also mist the glass as she draws even closer and looks upon the road. Guy is making his way along the street, a small, wounded bull with uncertain gait and startled eyes. His shoulders dip menacingly at those who pass by him. He appears to ignore acquaintances who touch their hats in salute.

"Puzzling?" I ask, but I know she needs no encouragement. Even with the distraction of Guy, she will not be shaken from this quest.

"That Mr. Guy's slate was also clean."

Now she turns to me and I feel her warm breath upon my cheek. My eyes remain on Guy who turns, blundering, into the pathway toward the house.

"I can't explain." My voice — thin and curiously detached from the mouth that hosts it — gives me the odd notion that it is not only Helen who is owed this missing explanation, but also myself.

The first wisp of an answer comes not in words but in a sensation: a man's hot gasp on my neck, the bristling of my own hairs. Then I hear that voice — *you think you're better than us?* — and the weight of a trembling hand upon my arm. The queasy memory tumbles into the glitter of ambition in Guy's face at the Crossroads Tavern, and his question posed with equal parts timidity and excitement: *If you yourself were in my position, how would you proceed?*

"I knew Guy couldn't handle it."

"Handle what?"

"The memory of a crime committed by his own hand."

I weigh the explanation while Guy's footsteps scuff upon the gravel before the house. It is perhaps a half-truth. The rest is murkier, a sense that I am already covered in the grime of other men's desires, that I am, and always will be, the natural receptacle of sin. "It's fate, that's all," I add feebly as the thud of the slamming front door vibrates through the house.

"It's my crime, not yours," she says, and I feel the warmth of her hand upon my arm. I can't disentangle any meaning from her words, but the implied union of souls and her touch recalls me to the promise between us, a vow unforced and unsullied, and soon to go before a priest. Uneasiness itches like ten dozen grubs crawling upon my flesh. The upcoming ceremony feels like the laying of finest silk upon carrion. I remember how my fingers puckered up folds of Helen's nightdress at the Crossroads Tavern, only to be distracted by . . . what? The business at hand? Or something else? It was surely my own unfitting which intervened when my longings came close to reaching their goal. A sullied cloak of other men's desires lies between Helen and I.

An animal yell, mighty and terrifying, comes from the hallway. Only as it dies away do I recognize the sound of my own name.

CHAPTER TWENTY-FOUR

Guy

My head is bursting, and I scarce know what words will come. Bartholomew follows me obediently enough into my study. The soft metred creak of his footfalls, the implied innocence of that smooth yet worried face, enrages me even more.

I make my way around the desk and stand behind it, stooping toward him, knuckles upon its surface. "So, I will be the very wellspring of pleasure to Eliza? True affection is sure to follow comfort?"

"Sir?" His eyes search me like a young deer sniffing a fern.

"Your words!" I yell, leaning harder upon my fists to prevent the tremble of rage.

"Things did not go well with Miss Eliza?"

"The sting of her hand is upon my face."

He tilts his head regretfully and sighs.

"You don't seem surprised."

He shrugs. "She is her father's daughter."

"Meaning?"

He gives an embarrassed smile. "She means to secure the best and most comfortable of everything for herself with the least effort."

The earnestness of his expression, his wide blue eyes, his hands outstretched, all begin to drain my moral outrage. I have to remind myself of his duplicity. He seemed absolutely certain of my success with Eliza before the act was committed; now he is far too quickly resigned to my failure, so quickly resigned indeed that it is impossible to believe he was ever as confident as he pretended. "You told me that the young do not look beyond the season they are in."

The reproach seems childlike upon my lips. The stoop in my shoulders that felt like an animal preparing to charge seems now like a self-pitying cringe. How many times has this young rogue seen the soft flesh quivering behind my shell of authority? How many times has anger and sternness melted to give way to the most abject of pleas? Whether it's because he knows of the cowardice underlying my ambition or because I have stooped to take from him the comforts of the seabound, Bartholomew unmans me by his presence.

"So I hoped," he says, looking genuinely bewildered. "But, in any case, you have control of her estates." He approaches the opposite side of the desk, almost within arm's reach. "This was your real motivation, after all: Cupers Cove. For the next eighteen months you can equip your expeditions as you see fit without scrimping or reference to a higher authority."

"Do you think I have involved myself in the foulest of all crimes for eighteen months' worth of pennies?" My lips tremble, and a sudden grief ushers forth a glimpse of one of my dreams: Eliza with her moist scales and her soft lips under my covers, the sweetest kernel of devotion aching and expanding into unspeakable bliss. This is my Eliza, pure spirit and unspoiled by the original from whom my imagination conjured her.

"Why don't you try again in a few weeks? She is still in deep mourning now."

"Eliza Egret is worthless!" The words surprise me. Am I really so unchivalrous? I feel the sudden need to explain myself. "She is not the woman I believed her to be. That's all. Cupers Cove is merely a trap."

"How so?"

This question, like all others from Bartholomew, sounds like pure innocence. But I've been here before and I feel the subtle, well-oiled machinery of persuasion sliding into motion.

"I may grow the colony, farm the land, explore the interior, and harvest the fish. But after eighteen months any expansion will be curtailed, as Eliza is sure to cut me off, and the venture will be sure to crumble." Through the rushing in my ears I hear the tramp of many feet through the brush; see the pick and the shovel, the yell of *eureka*! Such an untrodden expanse so far from the society of men is bound to hold mysteries under its rough soil. It is exactly where the gods of nature would keep their private hoard, daring only the valiant and the noble. "I need eighteen years and not eighteen months," I find myself murmuring. "The whole plan banked upon Mrs. Egret's estate in perpetuity." The rush in my ears has grown to a rumble. I'm suddenly aware that each hoop I go through to attain an increase in support for Cupers Cove merely opens up a hunger for more. Didn't I know this before? I remember Bartholomew's talk of ladders. The rungs, he told me, are climbed not in foreknowledge of all consequences but one at a time, and in ever-increasing hope.

"But you have time now to work on a plan for more permanent backing," he tells me. I look up to see his eyes flickering with intelligence — thoughts he will no doubt take his time over before venturing. I think of the black crime of which Bartholomew has already made me a part — a crime of ultimate futility unless followed up by even worse; the rumble in my ears grows into a wave of anger. What is it he would have me do next?

"What does that silence mean?" I demand, feeling the twitch of fury reach my fingertips.

"Nothing." His watery blue eyes mock me with false innocence.

"You were thinking something. Out with it!"

Eliza's slap has come down upon my cheek once more. A secret delight and a terror have merged upon the sting — the child-like impulse for disproportionate revenge. My imagination now bids me follow its course, to hear the very words of its unfolding upon Bartholomew's lips, and to be upon that luxurious balcony of sin where the action can be contemplated from the safety of vicariousness. As Bartholomew and I both know, there is only one means by which Mrs. Egret's estate could become mine in perpetuity, only one route through which I could receive, as he puts it, "permanent backing."

"As administrator of Eliza's inheritance, I am also her heir presumptive. Isn't that correct?"

"I suppose so," he says. His noncommittal shrug frustrates me. I want to jab him hard.

"How much would you want this time?"

"Mr. Guy, I have to take my leave." He nods at me as though I am to be humoured, and — sly dog that he is — even feigns trepidation as he begins to withdraw from the table. Raising his price, of course! The need to hear his real answer becomes almost painfully urgent.

"How much?"

"I have to leave," he repeats, opening his hands in the same infuriating gesture — the most innocent of demons!

Don't think, I tell myself. *Thought is the enemy of action.* I clamber as fast as I can over the table, leap and suddenly I'm upon him, fingers digging into the flesh beneath his collar, twisting the fabric. Books and papers fall and scatter from my desk to the floor, pushed off by my unsupported shoes. I fall upon the other side, on top of Bartholomew, knees upon his chest, hands burrowing into his collar like the teeth of a bull terrier worrying its quarry.

He squirms beneath me, and tries to roll, but I have him pinned. "You would have me murder again, you dog!"

"No!" he protests, wriggling, his fingers upon mine, trying to prize them from his collar.

"Name your price and be done with it!"

"Madman!"

This time he turns so quickly I am thrown. He's on his feet looking down upon me, his eyes blinking in horror. I want to tear that mask of virtue from him, to root inside and pull the quivering beast of dark intent from his heart, force it to speak its unholy desires. But I'm out of breath and he is backing off toward the doorway, hand reaching to his injured throat. In a moment more and without another word he is gone.

My plans to follow fizzle and die. As I turn onto my palms and begin rising rather painfully — a muscle in my back is yelping a protest — I hear a whispered exchange and the slamming of the front door. They are gone and will not return. Bartholomew has taken the dark intent with him to some unknown destination, hopefully not the same destination to which I am bound. Pulling myself upright against the rim of my table, a sudden clarity descends. The dark intent is still with me, grotesque and quivering. But it is shackled by a threat that is quite new: if I were to act now, it is only I who will be responsible.

Cupers Cove, my dreams of expansion, the tramping of expeditions into the interior all begin to fade in importance. I will go through the motions, of course, but the venture will wither along with one crime which I mean to disown, and the thought of another which will remain uncommitted. In the airless study, amid papers and books strewn underfoot,

only the faintest and most mournful of siren calls survives —
a memory of golden hair, the vague taste of salt rising and
falling on my tongue, and the foamy hiss of Eliza's skin
sliding against the sheets.

CHAPTER TWENTY-FIVE

Bartholomew

"CAN YOU REALLY HEAR the mermaids whisper?"

Helen's voice is so soft, my mind so crowded with present arrangements and recent occurrences — a sovereign for the priest, the witness we failed to provide, the sting from Guy's fingernails upon my neck — that I'm not sure I've caught her words correctly.

"What? What was that you said?" I tilt my head for the answer but keep my eyes fixed above the altar and upon the silver cross hanging in the misty shaft of light which aims like a sword through the blue stained glass.

"Do the mermaids really whisper in the darkness as the oceans roll upon the endless sands? Is the voluptuous moon really four times its usual size?"

"Is that what I told you?"

"Yes."

"Oh." I turn to the vestry archway where an ancient, crooked man with a broom — presumably the witness the priest said he could find for us — appears and slowly nods his gnarled head in my direction.

"And that the atmosphere hangs like honey tinged with cinnamon and clove."

"Yes," I say, returning my gaze to the cross.

"So it's true?"

"What? Oh, figuratively, yes."

"It isn't true, then," she says, resigned. "You better tell me what it *is* like."

I turn to her now and see her dark eyes full upon me. Her fingers skimming across the incense-fragranced pew take hold of mine, and something heavy inside me becomes feather-light and flips over, landing dizzily off-kilter. It takes awhile to see what has happened. The request, drably enough put, is a simple invitation to tell the truth, but it does not come with any withdrawal of commitment, nor with any threat of penalty should the answer displease.

"Cold, damp, windy, and grey," I tell her.

"Thank you," she says with a squeeze of my fingers, and for the second or third time since leaving Guy's home I feel the rank and grimy overcoat of other men's desires and ambitions begin to loosen from my neck and shoulders.

"And the people?"

"Best steered clear from. That's why we are aiming for a new plantation some miles to the north."

"Do you have a bad name there, Bartholomew?"

The question — its extraordinary insight — takes me aback.

"Yes," I say after a pause. "I have a bad name there."

"Then you should change it. We need a fresh beginning."

Puzzled by the suggestion, by its correlation to a thought of my own, I watch the elderly witness put aside his broom very slowly and carefully, and then make his tortoise-like progress toward us. I find the cross reclaiming my eyes, this time with a question — *what have you to offer this girl?* The four opposing paths comprise the eternal sign of choice. I am as damned as any man can be. I have taken a life. I have involved this young woman in the process. Could I at least not leave her alone?

Her fingers remain on mine and squeeze once more. "I told you it was my crime, not yours, and I meant it."

My heart tumbles two beats into one. I turn to see a surprising intensity in her gaze. Is it not some proof of union when a woman can dive unaided into the mind of a man and view the contents clearly enough to emerge with the one thought that plagues him the most?

"I was the one with cause to hurt him and I was the one with cause to protect him. He was my father."

The intelligence robs me of breath. A draft sweeps through the half-lit interior and I turn to see the cross trembling upon its wires. We are both damned then. The idea seems to make things better. I think of the night in the Crossroads Tavern again, of my fingers caressing the folds of her nightdress. If Helen is sullied also we could be like snakes together in the pit, damned by the world but kind to each other.

The ancient man, his shoulders bent like a question

mark, sits down on the front pew on the opposite aisle. His hands — pale but blotchy with growths — tremble with the years. I wonder how time might judge us.

The priest, black and white like a magpie in mourning, emerges from the vestry at last, a record book flapping in his hand. As we rise my chest thumps like a cartwheel turning over stone. I haven't given the priest my name yet; we've exchanged payment and details of time and place only.

"What name should I choose?" I whisper to Helen urgently.

The ancient man half turns. Do his eyes narrow in suspicion?

"Take the name of Mrs. Egret's husband. She calls him upright and daring."

I wince at a perceived irony. But when I meet her steady, earnest gaze, I find she means it after all. "Nicholas it is. And the surname?"

We shuffle out from the pew and, meeting our witness in the aisle, take the few short paces slowly together to the altar.

"Your name, sir?" asks the priest, quill and record book at the ready.

A full name comes to me immediately and I push it away. The choices continue spinning like wheel spokes in motion, a constant, never-ending exchange. Why was the first idea repugnant? The prickle of urgency crawls up my arms.

"Nicholas," I say to buy time.

Grey eyebrows raise, and the priest gives a short sigh of impatience.

"Your full name please."

Exchange of crime, exchange of guilt, exchange of respon-sibility, the spinning wheel seems to say, a one-way exchange all the way, save for a small portion of stock, enough for two boats and the charge of a couple of men. Why not at least take his name in payment? The wheel arriving full circle again prods me with the inevitable word, and this time there is no excuse for hesitation and no time for rethought.

"Guy," I tell him. "Nicholas Guy."

CHAPTER TWENTY-SIX

Helen

October 1612

GULLS CIRCLE THE SWELLING sail of the Cupers Cove ship as it disappears around the headland. The laughter of the birds, faint but persistent, reaches me as the breeze unexpectedly changes direction, tugging at my clothes with its warm fingers.

Like wolves padding around their prey the questions come closer each time we have contact with John Guy's colony.

"Where's Mr. Nicholas Guy this time?" Colston asked me an hour ago, weighing his pronunciation of the name with an unnatural and skeptical emphasis. "I was hoping to meet him just once before the end of the season." His strong, meaty hand gripped our wharf in proprietary fashion, his head cocked to the side. "Is he exploring the interior *again*?"

The Cupers Cove men know well enough there is some mystery. Perhaps they imagine there is no such plantation owner, that I alone direct Jake and Matthew, our men, and Sarah, Matthew's young sister. Perhaps they have postulated that the fictitious husband, "Mr. Nicholas Guy," is some form of protection. Were it to become generally known the plantation was run by a woman, perhaps, some authority could be invoked to confiscate these grounds, the houses, the boats, and wharf. It is fair reasoning, of course, and the fear they seem to sense makes it hard for them to leave us alone.

Mr. John Guy has apparently said nothing all this time; according to his men he has no knowledge of a distant cousin here, but does not deny the possibility. I can easily imagine his murmured and red-faced response as he busies himself with some urgent task.

Soon Guy will be gone again, leaving his community to fend for itself or collapse into disorder in the cold months ahead. We'll be safer from Cupers Cove too when winter closes upon us. But next year worries me, and the years after that. How long can I keep Bartholomew from sight without their resentment spilling into aggression? I'm afraid that like a badly stitched garment, this island's coast will become tattered with the dangling threads of suspicion and disharmony. I fear the twin demons of hunger and distrust, more so today than ever before, as I've felt a change within me this morning — more than mere nausea or dizziness this time, more than an absence of blood. We are weaving the world afresh, Bartholomew and I, and Matthew, Jake, and Sarah, and in some ways it's a ragged enough beginning. Our very first act has been to dissemble.

I turn from the ocean, intending to climb through the bush to Bartholomew's hideout, but something — a flicker or spark of movement — catches the edge of my vision and compels me to turn back to the waves. And there I see it.

The reddening sun over my shoulder skims over the water's surface, setting the wave-dance on fire. Each ocean ridge peaks slowly, holds itself up as though yearning to attain some nameless bliss, and then tumbles joyously into its sisters to build afresh. I think of my own half-sister, Eliza, the merciless tug of my hair, the names I was called as a child. Did she know I was her kin? Such fury must come from somewhere. But this is not the way it has to be. Sister can be friends with sister, brother with brother, and cove with cove if it comes to that.

The constant movement I witness seems to transfer, rippling in my belly now. It is surely too early to kick, yet life will either have expression or die. It is time to tell Bartholomew. In the meeting of two peaks a stone's throw away I see a curious swirl of foam, the hint of a dipping wet back, and then the shiver of a tail, ribbed like a fan and catching the sun's sparkle. I wait to see if it will reappear, but the waves heave, peak, tumble, then reform. Nothing but foam shows above the surface. The impression, nevertheless, has stirred a desire for the magic of surprise, a belief that many possibilities lurk beneath the surface of things.

As I turn at last and begin tramping up the incline,

coarse, low-lying bushes tug at my skirts. Bartholomew emerges unexpectedly from a group of trees much lower on the hill than usual. His face is rather white, his eyes twitchy and red as is often the case when a ship from Cupers Cove is sighted. He scrabbles down the hill toward me.

"It's gone," I say, "you're safe."

He looks not toward the ocean but at me, and I know that expression, the unnatural passivity of a mask with the suggestion of turbulence beneath. It is the same expression I witnessed in the Crossroads Tavern when I returned to tell him that I would after all murder my master, the same one I saw again when he climbed Mr. Guy's stairs to the attic space where I had prepared myself for the mummering. It is the expression of change and second thought.

"Yes," he breathes unsmiling, his gaze flicking toward the ocean.

"So, until the next time, you can relax."

Silent, rather dishevelled like a young scarecrow, he stares at me.

"That's what you want?" I ask.

"No."

He turns his head, scans the brush dotting the hill, the woods above.

"What then?"

"Maybe I should take my chances."

I wait for more.

His gaze returns to me, and then looks over my shoulder at the ocean.

"Maybe I should stop hiding."

A smile steals into my face. He sees this and nods.

"Well, let's go home," I tell him, taking his arm. "I've got something to tell you."

CHAPTER TWENTY-SEVEN

Bartholomew

How BLIND THE COURAGE of daylight seems when the clarity of night descends! Roof planks rattle. Insulating moss sighs as the searching winds shift. I can so easily imagine the stealthy approach of men from every direction. I can almost hear them scuff around the tilt where Jake and Matthew sleep. I can hear the stones skittering as they clamber over the rocks on the seaward side of our enclosure. Each creep, each whoosh of grass, each twig that snaps brings them closer to us, to the hot breath upon my neck again. But this time would be much worse. The heat of desire will have rolled into the blade of revenge. And since Helen's news, there is so much more to lose.

"Maybe I should stop hiding," were the words thrown carelessly into the late afternoon. The fact that I am to be a father has conspired to weave this careless suggestion into a vow. It's no longer just us. A parent's shame will weigh heavy upon the shoulders of a daughter or son. How can I back out now? How can a growing child watch as his father retreats into the woods and his mother lies to cover the tracks of her husband? The promise of new life demands the example of pride, and I have trapped myself, it seems, into providing it.

Helen moans beside me and shifts first onto her back and then onto her side, facing away from me. I feel the warm pat of her hand on my leg — my compensation — as she turns. Soon, another life will have sprouted between us, and my dreamless brain buzzes with the sights and sounds of the cradle: the bald infant, with red face and tiny fists shaking their ineffectual protests; the growing child tottering on unsteady feet, new curls reaching thin and fernlike from the disappearing dome of its head.

The first suggestion I might be wavering from my accidental vow drew from Helen a response so withering I believed myself to be in the nursery once more. The idea that I stop hiding was, to Helen, a sign of growing up. It must have seemed natural to her that I would falter from this resolve at least once, natural that I, like her, would try to climb back upon the beast of maturity without delay.

"Don't be silly," she said when I told her that to the Cupers Cove people I am still a criminal, and must be careful. She was crouching above the cooking pot which perched firmly upon the stove-circle. The words, so utterly confident in their scorn, might have been addressed to the carrots and turnips had they possessed the effrontery to pose as the deadliest of poisons.

"Why do you find it so hard to believe?" I asked, heat rising to my cheek. "Remember I stole the pendant. Remember it was I who conceived our plan against Mr. Egret." I nearly added it was also I who carried it out, but I didn't want to remind her. "That's behind me now, of course." I winced at the note of pomposity in my voice. "I'm reformed. But in my time I have done many things which lay far beyond the dictates of the law."

She raised her eyes in my direction. A sad, bitter smile played upon her face.

"Did you kill your own father?"

"No," I said, and my lips tightened like those of a scolded boy aware of the many hoops of knowledge that separate him from his teacher.

"Then you are a novice, and, thank God, you will always remain so."

She raised the spoon to her lips, tasted, and then went back to stirring.

NOW, WITH HER DOZING form beside me, I long to be that reckless youth who once shocked her with his thievery. There was a fire in my gut then, a quality that was unpredictable even to me. I believe I found some sort of comfort, as well as endless self-flattery, in the notion that a reckless, fearsome spirit dwelt within me. But now things are different. Once the flames of inner discord have been quenched, all fear must turn outward for its cause. To the man who no longer intimidates himself, the world is suddenly full of shadows.

How long ago Bristol seems! Lying open-eyed, I once again conjure the memory of Helen and I sitting together by the fire near the Broad Quay, her warm curiosity, her innocent need for adventure, nudging me along a path of lies invented moment by moment, bend by bend. It was delicious indeed when I slipped my hand inside my pocket, felt the hot gold against my fingers, then drew the pendant out by the chain. I remember how it rotated slowly, its emeralds and diamonds dancing in the light of the flame, how Helen's gasp came as though spouting from somewhere deep inside the earth, a wellspring of pure emotion yet to be defined.

Was I only kidding myself? I wonder. Was I not as I believed myself, the wizard who skips over the rocks of mundane existence, dazzling the onlooker with each nimble dance move beyond the shackles of morality? Was I always as Helen sees me now — a boy forced into crime by the simple desire to survive, escape, and prosper?

"There was nothing so special about your sins, Bartholomew," she told me, stirring her stew. I received this news like a cannonball to the chest. "They were merely of necessity and circumstance. It's time to forget them."

I wanted to ask her what she had thought of me that night in Bristol when she sat by the dockside fire, hands over her mouth, tears streaming down her face. *Were you not*, the words almost rise into my mouth, *just a little impressed?* Instead I sat quietly, listening to the wind and waiting for dinner, trying in vain to ward off visions of myself as the future will no doubt encounter me: a hard-working man with thickening waist and balding head; a man of care and constant worry, vigilant of fever and famine as his children grow; an aging man with back bent from digging roots from the earth; a man of swollen joints who loves the simplest and most modest of pleasures — the puff of tobacco, the heat of an outdoor fire in September. This is not how it was meant to be, yet this is where I am. The flint of danger and the cloak of mystery were decoys against this simple truth: I am ordinary.

This is what Helen believes, and for a moment I am almost ready to agree with her, almost ready to embrace the idea as welcome. Peril and crime are exhausting, after all. But a change in the wind and the distant rattle of planks scoop fresh danger into my mind. Helen does not know. How can she? Men are capable of anything when they fear their true desires may be exposed. We are not safe at all.

CHAPTER TWENTY-EIGHT

Guy

THE ROPE COMES DOWN upon my desk with a triumphant slap. Colston smiles at me like a man who has just won a fortune in a game of cards.

"What this?" I ask quietly, laying down my quill. I wonder why the candle flame should quiver in response to my own hushed voice though it remained entirely unaffected by Colston's swiping movements. My gestures, my words — everything I do these past few days — has been measured and soft; I won't let anything disturb the delicate thread of my plans. Repairs must be completed to my returning ship on time. There must be no dispute with the men. A superstitious part of me won't raise my voice for fear it may provoke the weather to unleash its random vengeance. So delicate is the balance, so great the need to return, I hardly dare breathe.

"This is the noose that will hang him."

Only now do I notice that the rope on my desk forms a loop. Raucous laughter and shouting from somewhere outside grows apace, then dies away.

"What are you talking about, Colston?"

The question, of course, is a lie. I know what it all means, but I am waiting for the fog of panic to clear.

"It *is* Bartholomew in the plantation to the north. Somehow he has made his way back. We should return immediately so we can be upon him even before he wakes."

I rise from my chair and step out from the desk.

"What makes you think it is him?"

"We designated Browne as a watch. He stayed in the cove and waited until after we left. When we picked him up around the next headland, he confirmed it. Bartholomew emerged from the woods the moment he thought our ship gone."

"I gave you no such authorization." Circling the tiny room, I feel like a fly trapped in a web, twitching for freedom.

"It's a minor detail, sir. We *have* him!" With this, he beats his fist so hard upon the desk the noose jumps half an inch. I turn from him. "He's within our grasp. The man who ruined our crop, the villain who escaped your custody!"

My back is still turned for the moment, but I can hear Colston panting in anticipation. What would be the easiest course? I ask myself. The answer seems simple enough. Let them have their revenge. Let them string him up. He may babble his story about Bristol. He may tell them I released him voluntarily on the ship, that I later gave him stock in the Company in return for his crimes, and that I provided, though reluctantly, passage on my returning ship to the cove in which he now dwells. But this is one occasion when he would not be believed. Everyone knows that a condemned man will say anything to avoid the drop, and the men hate Bartholomew so deeply, no amount of his golden rhetoric would hide the evil they perceive. Still, something holds me from giving the word.

"Quickly, sir," he tells me. "The men are eager!"

"I'm sure they are, Colston," I say trying to gauge the direction of the hubbub, guessing the men must be down by the wharf, "I'm sure they are." I turn to face his deepening frown, his shoulders hunched over my desk, his thick hands spread upon its surface, fingers twitching by the noose. "Unfortunately, the regulations by which we govern ourselves are still crystal clear. Capital crimes are brought back to England."

Pushing himself off from the desk, he breathes a sigh and smiles. "Who would know the difference? He is a fugitive!"

"*I* would know, Colston."

He watches me for a moment, to check I am in earnest. Looking inward, I do the same, listening to my heartbeat, to the sound of a man who wants nothing more than to leave Newfoundland for good, and who has just rearranged every expectation, including his own, to make the delay of argument and rebellion far more likely.

"You mean to stand in our way?"

"No," I say quietly.

He drops his shoulders in relief and moves forward to the desk to claim his rope. My hand reaches out as though to receive. He tilts his head then, with a moment's hesitation, hands over the noose. My fingers grip the dry hemp.

"I don't mean to 'stand in your way,' as you put it. I mean to stop you and have you clear any such thought from your head." I lift the rope, not quite knowing why, until I feel the fibres ruffle my hair and the noose dropping heavily around my own neck like a displaced halo. Colston stares at me bewildered. "If you use this on anybody," I say softly, "you will have to use it on me first."

Exasperated, Colston raises his hand to his hip and anchors it there.

"And if you're thinking of waiting until I leave before you move, don't," I say. "There are ways of knowing if foul deeds have been committed, even from England. I am quite prepared to make the Company aware of my misgivings about the Colony's intentions."

"You owe your men an explanation, sir," he says, disparagement, perhaps even disgust in his face as he looks upon my heavy necklace. I remove the noose slowly and keep it hanging from my fingers.

·"Have you or your men seen any mermaids recently, Colston?"

He bristles, standing upright; I hear a swift inhalation.

"What does that mean?"

I think of withdrawing the remark, but I spy the flinch of fear beneath his pride and suspect he may at any moment look for an excuse to back off. In the silence, I trace through the path of my decision. If I left things as they were, Bartholomew would likely be dead before sunrise. I would have ensured against delays in leaving; in fact, I would have earned myself the heartiest of send-offs. As it is, my last hours here will tick slowly away under the pall of suspicion. There must be some very powerful reason for me to have spoken and acted as I have done. A distant shriek comes from down on the wharf, accompanied by more laughter and the beginnings of a chant, the words of which I do not catch. With the ugly knot of sound comes the beginning of an answer: there was a part of me once, an upright, noble part which believed in meeting the world face-on. It was this part, and not the rest of me, who had originally sought to woo Eliza Egret. Gradually, it seems, this rock of decency sank into the mire of subterfuge. The cost of my ambition was foisted upon another, just as the cost of this rabble's desire has been foisted upon another. That this object happens to be one and the same makes this new hint of reclamation more promising than I deserve.

"I will not allow this man to pay for my sins, or the sins of the colony," I say at last, and as I speak I watch his expression fold into defeat. Even the candlelight reveals the subtle lines of guilt and self-realization. "Calm them down, Colston. Get them to see sense. Tell them they have wives now, and that wives need husbands, not outlaws, which is what this act would make them."

He gives a long, sickly sigh, turns, and leaves. The door opens to animal shouts that soften only slightly as it clumps shut. To Bristol I will return, I tell myself, a duller man than I once hoped I would be, but one who has finally, and perhaps belatedly, relearned one lesson so easily lost in the byways and vicissitudes of experience and self-justifications. Tonight I remembered the difference between right and wrong.

EPILOGUE

Bartholomew

March 1613

His arms push back, crooked at the elbow. His head rolls upon its wrinkled neck while my hands hover over him like hesitant doves. Sarah's own neat movements take over quickly, lifting the creature into her own chest, and moving him in a careful up-and-down dance. A spluttering moan, a protest perhaps, gives way to one long, rising note, which falls at last into that timeless rhythm of lament with which all women and men greet their entry into the world.

His eyes, almost closed like those of a bat, seem to open and stay upon me for just a second. His fight-fisted arms batter against Sara's shoulder as the girl glides the baby down into Helen who lays spent, hair drenched with sweat, chest heaving with effort and pain, eyes moist with something other than this, and mouth puckering as though to receive a longed for succor. She looks at me too as her long fingers move over the translucent flesh of our newborn: it is the rarest of looks, one of those that link together a lifetime, making all that is lost in pain and confusion, all that is feared, no more terrible than a few wilted stalks in a chain of daisies. It is a look that says: *this is why we are here; we will always remember this moment.*

It's the right time for both of us, I think, and the right time for the child. Providence breathed upon us yesterday, when Sara's brother, Matthew, returned from the wharf, ax in his left hand, a sack dangling from his right. "The men from Cupers Cove have been looking for seals close by," he mumbled in that way of his, as though words threatened to fetter the free running of his thoughts. Knowing the mistress of the cove was expecting, he told me, their womenfolk prepared something. My heart rolled a warning at the idea of a gift from Cupers Cove and I peered inside before taking it into Helen.

Indoors, the sackcloth whispered as together we drew the object out. A nest of finely interwoven twigs — more like something created by a giant bird than by the nimble fingers of women — was filled inside with smaller sacks of seeds: turnip, carrot, and pea. Helen held my eye, a slight smile playing upon her lips. I stroked her hand and moved outdoors.

Winter still crystallized the cove, hanging over the wharf rails and glistening on the dark hills and cliffs. But the sun was slowly warming the land. I could almost hear the move-ment of the roots and stems as they pushed through the earth and opened tongue-like buds of palest green. Light scattered over the waves that undulated like long stretches of fabric held at either end of a room and fluttered. In these movements I seemed to behold a perpetual, joyful dance of fin and tail. This, I found myself thinking, could indeed be a place of security, a place of love. At the very least, our time had come to live in faith.

ACKNOWLEDGEMENTS

I would like to thank publishers Garry Cranford, Margo Cranford, and Jerry Cranford for their belief in this novel, and everyone at Flanker Press for their positive ethos and attention to detail. Many thanks to editor Ed Kavanagh for sharing his insight and knowledge. My appreciation to The Newfoundland and Labrador Arts Council which supported this project with a writing grant. And thanks, as always, to my wife, Maura Hanrahan, and to my daughter Jemma to whom this book is quite fittingly dedicated.

PAUL BUTLER is the author of several criti-
cally acclaimed novels including *Hero, 1892,
NaGeira, Easton's Gold, Easton,* and *Stoker's
Shadow.* His work has appeared on the
judges' lists for *Canada Reads,* the *Relit*
longlist, and he was a winner in the
*Government of Newfoundland and Labrador
Arts and Letters Awards* four times between
2003 and 2008. A graduate of Norman
Jewison's Canadian Film Centre, Butler has
written for the *Globe and Mail, The Beaver,
Books in Canada, Atlantic Books Today,* and
Canadian Geographic, and has also con-
tributed to CBC Radio, local and national. He
lives in St. John's.